PRAISE FOR
BRIAN M. WIPRUD
AND
CROOKED

"Unique and thoroughly enjoyable. While comparisons to other authors are inevitable they are also unnecessary. Wiprud has a voice all his own and it's one I look forward to hearing more of. This should be on everyone's 'to buy' list."
—*Crimespree*

"Wiprud's engaging, hard-boiled style draws readers into both the art world and the underworld of New York, and his colorful cast keeps things moving with wit to spare—especially the plucky lead.... The journey is a thrilling one, with an ending even the most astute readers won't see coming."
—*Publishers Weekly*

"Clever. Outrageous. Pure fun ... *Crooked* is hard hitting with no holds barred, and the characters are worth meeting—at least in print."
—*BookLoons*

STUFFED

A *Seattle Times* bestseller
A *January Magazine* Holiday Gift Pick

"A dizzying and sometimes dangerous romp... Wiprud's imagination runs wild here, and he skillfully brings the reader along.... His protagonist's frequent and eccentric musings about everything from the joy of cheap moose heads to the pain of parking signs add to the lighthearted tone." —*Publishers Weekly*

"*Stuffed* marks the long-awaited (especially by readers and reviewers who like their humorous mysteries clever and artful rather than just zany or wisecracking) return of crime-solving New York taxidermist Garth Carson, whose debut in 2002's *Pipsqueak* was a cause for much pleasure."
—*Chicago Tribune*

"For all its eccentricities, *Stuffed* is imbued with a sense of realism that makes this offbeat mystery all the more pleasurable.... Wiprud's skill at creating believable characters and realistic scenes, no matter how weird, makes *Stuffed* shine."
—*South Florida Sun-Sentinel*

"Often harrowing, at times macabre, and always original. Wiprud twangs funny bones I never knew I had." —T. Jefferson Parker,
author of *California Girl*

"The Nick and Nora of Taxidermy meet the Maltese Falcon...er...Squirrel in another crazy, funny mystery from Brian M. Wiprud."
—Sparkle Hayter

"No *Pipsqueak*—this is a muscular adventure! Admirers of Donald Westlake and Elmore Leonard especially, though, will find much here to enjoy. Wiprud is definitely a writer to watch."
—*Mystery Ink*

"Zany [and] outrageous...This novel is highly recommended for readers who like quirky capers, or who simply remember sitting in front of TV cartoons for hours, never understanding the concept of the OFF button." —*January Magazine,* Best of 2002

"A very funny, well-plotted, and imaginative tale... Loopy cults, retro rage, a diabolical conspiracy, a black-sheep brother, it's all here...."
—*Booknews* from The Poisoned Pen

"Crime and taxidermy collide in this zany, zestfully told tale. Sublime comic storyteller Wiprud sets his mystery in a fictional New York City 'retro' subculture, full of zoot-suited hipsters, swing-loving horn players and other eccentric city dwellers.... Quirky characters, slapstick situations, and clever writing full of sharp visual images make this novel a thrill a minute."
—*Romantic Times,* Top Pick!

Also by Brian M. Wiprud

PIPSQUEAK

STUFFED

CROOKED

SLEEP
with the
FISHES

BRIAN M. WIPRUD

A Dell Book

Dell

SLEEP WITH THE FISHES
A Dell Book / October 2006

Published by Bantam Dell
A Division of Random House, Inc.
New York, New York

This is a work of fiction. Names, characters, places, and
incidents either are the product of the author's imagination or
are used fictitiously. Any resemblance to actual persons, living
or dead, events, or locales is entirely coincidental.

Dell is a registered trademark of Random House, Inc.,
and the colophon is a trademark of Random House, Inc.

ISBN-13: 978-0-440-24313-7
ISBN-10: 0-440-24313-0

Printed in the United States of America
Published simultaneously in Canada

www.bantamdell.com

OPM   10 9 8 7 6 5 4 3 2 1

Dedicated to Dr. William K. Runyeon, my uncle, who died while fishing for shad in the Delaware River last June. A singular man and angler, he is much missed.

This tale is also dedicated in some small part to the memory of Frederick Arbogast Schmudt, late of Porters Lake Hunting & Fishing Club, who was oft heard to admonish "Fish often, fish well, and avoid lonely, one-eyed bootleggers."

We should not be too hasty in bestowing either our praise or censure on mankind, since we shall often find such a mixture of good and evil in the same character, that it may require a very accurate judgment and a very elaborate inquiry to determine on which side the balance turns.

—Henry Fielding

SLEEP
with the
FISHES

Front wheels locked sideways, the Volkswagen Rabbit spun backward, sparks flaring as it snapped the cable guide rail and flipped over the embankment. After a few protracted somersaults, the puckered chassis slammed roof-first onto a pile of boulders. Shattered safety glass rained from the windows and snakes of fire raced up rivulets of gas, igniting the engine. The dark ravine was suddenly dancing with light from the blaze.

Headlights flashed above, and a white Mercury Marquis pulled to a stop on the road. A man in a jogging suit and windbreaker emerged and walked casually to the edge of the embankment, the blaze below reflecting tiny campfires in his eyes. The whole underside of the Rabbit was afire now, and the man figured it would only be a minute before she blew.

"Adios," he smirked, tugging on one ear absently, turning back toward his Mercury.

A cough sounded in the ravine, and the man froze. Looking both ways along the road, he pulled a small revolver from his waistband. He cocked it, then stepped back to the edge of the ravine and peered down the embankment.

"Oh, that's just friggin' beautiful," he moaned. A bearded man lay sprawled on the rocks below, steam rising from his coughs into the cold night air.

"Oh my God," drawled a woman's voice. "There's been an accident!" The man wheeled around and staggered with surprise.

"What the hell?" He quickly slipped the gun back in his waistband. "Angel! What the...Jesus! What're you doin' in my backseat?" he sputtered.

Her painted face twisted into a scowl as she emerged from the blanket she'd been hiding under.

"Well, big shot, mind tellin' me what you always goin' out late at night for?" she shrieked. "Sure, you keep sayin' 'I got business, Angel.' Business my butt. I'm here to find out who she is."

"Who?" he yelled, throwing his arms wide. "So help me, Angel, I oughta kill you for this!"

"Sid, I heard you talkin' tuh Johnny. You said somethin' about how you got 'an appointment with Sandra.'" Angel opened the car door and stepped out onto the pavement in her panty-hosed feet. "And what, for this tramp Sandra, you come all the way up here to Connecticut?" She tugged at her angora sweater.

Another cough echoed up the ravine, and Sid looked anxiously down at the stirring figure below.

"Well, are you just gonna walk back and forth there, flappin' your arms like a pigeon, or are y'gonna help the poor guy? Jeez, go on, hurry, he could be dying or something!" Angel wailed, leaning on the car and squeezing scarlet pumps onto her feet.

Flabbergasted and red-faced, Sid ogled his girl-friend's scarlet shoes and shook his head, trying to wake himself from this nightmare. Then he scrambled down the embankment to the victim. Peering at the flaming wreckage, he could see the arm of another victim protruding motionless from where the windshield used to be. He slipped the gun from his waist and put it to the bearded man's head.

"O.K., Evel Knievel, just keep your eyes and your mouth shut, and I'll save your sorry ass, you got that?" It didn't look like the poor schnook could make out much anyway. Probably wouldn't live. So he tugged, heaved, huffed, and puffed the bearded guy by the collar up to the shoulder of the road, dropping him none too gently.

"Angel—into the car." Sid wheezed harshly, his white pants and arms smeared with dirt and leaves. "We gotta go get help for this guy." He grabbed Angel by the arm and thrust her into the backseat.

"Hey!" Angel bleated. "What about—"

"Shuddup, already. We gotta hurry, get to a phone, get this guy an ambulance or somethin'." He could hear a truck shifting gears, a possible witness, coming up the hill. The Mercury's engine revved, its tires squealed, and it sped quickly away.

There was a whoosh like a sudden drumroll as the gasoline around the Rabbit caught fire. Shrieking flames burst the gas tank, and the bearded man's crumpled form was silhouetted by an ascending swirl of fire.

chapter **1**

"You jerks wanna know what you can do with your Witness Protection Program? Don't worry, I'll let you fill in that blank. Hey, I did a thing for you, I ratted out these guys. Look at me, I'm thirty-three years old—all I want is the short stint. And when I get out...Well, I been takin' care of myself this far. So it's this way: the Feds'll save a lot of green not havin' to babysit me my whole life. I want you to consider that when my sentence comes down—know what I'm talking about?"

Oh, the Feds had warned Sid about the dangers, that outside of the WPP he might well get chopped up and otherwise disemboweled by his former comrades in the Palfutti family. But before Sid decided to turn state's evidence, before he testified, he'd worked out another kind of deal. The rival Camuchi family had made arrangements with his shark of a lawyer to insure that Sid would rat out his confederates at their trials, and in such a way as to scuttle the Palfutti family once and for all. In return, the Camuchis would see to it that any Palfuttis that were not arrested as a result of his testimony were in no position to whack Sid. As a token of their confidence, they'd made a tidy $500,000 honorarium to the Sid Bifulco Defense Fund. The Camuchis were, in effect, buying up the Palfutti turf and rackets for a song.

And so with the deal from both the Feds and the Camuchis in his pocket, Sid took the stand. Days in the Trenton, New Jersey, courtroom were tense as a succession of Palfutti defendants gave Sid the evil eye. But Sid, a sinewy guy with salt-and-pepper hair, remained impassive. He seemed calm, confident, and matter-of-fact. Hours of scratchy recordings, expert testimony, and lawyers' charts filled the weeks. And of course there was the small matter of cross-examination.

"Mr. Bifulco, could you tell the court how you came upon the nickname 'Sleep'?" The defense attorney looked like a tall gray heron with a frog caught in his throat.

"Yeah, I could tell you." Sid laced his fingers into a teepee and focused his dark eyes beyond the rail of the witness box and onto the stenographer's red pumps.

"Could you elaborate for the jury, Mr. Bifulco?" The tall gray bird eyed the jury knowingly.

"Sure." Sid cleared his throat. "It's cause when I whacked a guy..."

"You mean when you murdered someone, don't you, Mr. Bifulco?"

"Yeah, that's what I said. When I *killed* a guy, I usually put him to sleep. First I sapped 'em, then I either, you know, suffocated 'em or injected 'em with procaine. Nice an' easy. No blood to clean up, no strugglin' or nothin'. Johnny Fest made funna me. Called me Sleep. So it stuck. See, Johnny was the kinda guy that liked a guy to know he was gettin' whacked, liked the guy to—"

"Mr. Bifulco! Could you do something for me? Could you please just try and concentrate on the question? Hmm?"

Directly across from the witness stand sat Bluto incarnate, a brooding hulk squeezed into a double-breasted suit. His name was Johnny Fest, a captain in the Palfutti family who moodily examined the ceiling and cracked his knuckles.

Every time Sid mentioned Johnny, defendant Fest popped a knuckle or two. It sounded like someone snapping ice trays and made it hard for Sid to keep his eyes on the stenographer's shoes.

"Could you tell us, Mr. Bifulco, how many people you personally 'put to sleep'—that is, *murdered*—in your career as a hoodlum?" The heron cocked an alarmed eye back at the jury.

"Sure. Something like ten," Sid lied, shrugging at the judge as if he'd accidentally run over a cat.

Confessing to murder didn't faze him. When you were part of a crew, such admissions—albeit mostly by implication—were not only commonplace but also necessary. A reputation for "doing a thing" maintained the respect and fear necessary for a fruitful career. Sid was only concerned that more than the paltry ten murders could be pinned on him, possibly pushing his parole eligibility into the next decade.

"Something like ten. 'Something like' ten murders." The heron ruffled his feathers, stretched his wings, and began to squawk. "*How can a person who can't even remember how many people he murdered remember who other people murdered?*"

Sid grinned bitterly and wondered how a guy like himself could get in such a jam over red high heels. He knew a lot of guys who had drinking problems, and then there were some who ended up with coke habits. Others couldn't successfully cheat on their wives, and had business meetings broken up by embarrassing confrontations. These guys got warnings, and then the next thing you knew they got popped. But Sid wasn't a heavy drinker, a coke dog, or sloppily married. For a single mob lieutenant, his vice seemed quite pedestrian: Bifulco liked women, and he had a particular overwhelming fondness for red shoes. It was the ladies in hot pumps who always seemed to make Sid lose his head and get in trouble.

Long knobby legs carried the defense attorney around and around the courtroom, and Mr. Bifulco was compelled to recount all of his ten murders, which he did matter-of-factly, if not rather absent-mindedly. Hands locked in a wigwam on his lap, Sid clamped his dark eyes on those shoes and tried to ignore the sound of ice trays cracking off to his left. He was just glad that the big gray bird hadn't wheeled an accusing hand at him and said, "So, Mr. Bifulco, isn't it true that you're a sucker for ladies in red shoes? That, in fact, you were once almost killed because of red shoes? That, in fact, your *downfall* was because of your love—or maybe I should say fetish?—for red shoes? Mr. Bifulco, please answer the question."

Sid's curse had plagued him since he was twelve. Saturday nights he and his pals would spy on couples steaming up car windows by the Passaic River bulkhead, Pulaski Skyway rusting and twinkling overhead. From within the upholstered shadows of the huge old Chevys, Oldsmobiles, and Buicks rocked mating rhythms. Faces were never seen, just glimpses of flesh, flashes of belt buckles, feet, pleated skirts, and hands, the jujitsu of love punctuated by muffled yelps, giggles, gasps, and curses. And eventually, there were shoes, women's shoes in the air, against the window where Sid's face was pressed. Sometimes the shoes fell off early, as soon as the feet went in the air, or before. Sometimes the shoes stayed on the whole time, pounding and clawing the glass at Sid's nose. It was a pair of shiny red high heels that finally overwhelmed Sid's pituitary. And when his father discovered the boy washing underwear in the sink, well, it was obvious that it was time to deal with Sid's sexual awakening. Removing his belt, Father Bifulco gave the lad a memorable beating.

That was only the first time red shoes got Sid in dutch. He had dodged the shoe bullet on several occasions. After a few years, and any number of encounters with amateur, semipro, and professional women, a stray red shoe was a common sight either in Sid's car or his apartment. Recording his conversations had been as easy as tossing a pair of red shoes with wireless mics into his white Mercury Marquis.

The Feds said he'd done a good job. The papers blared "COOL RAT." But the job was neither good nor cool. It was what Sid Bifulco, thirty-three years old, needed to do to save whatever he had left of a life ruined by a pair of flame-red suede pumps with transmitters in the heels. The Feds had taped over a hundred hours of conversation in which he and associates had discussed innumerable felonies, via shoes hidden under the front seat of his car.

In his deal with the prosecutors, Sid pulled down a twelve-year stint in exchange for putting his colleagues away for life—and he'd be eligible for parole in seven. What was left of the Palfutti crime family when Sid got through testifying against them was either absorbed by the New York crowd or dispatched by them, or both.

Nobody bothered Sid in prison because, well, you just don't tease a guy with ten notches in his gun. But he was hardly a cell-block heavy. He was a malefactor who rationalized his capital crimes as the humane approach to eliminating the jerks who'd "get whacked anyhow"—probably quite unpleasantly at the hands of Johnny Fest. Sid Bifulco was a wiseguy with sensibilities, whereas Johnny Fest's confrontational aesthetic might involve shoving a pigeon down a victim's throat, cutting off his dick, and throwing him from a twelve-story building.

Sid's victims had fatal car accidents, or they simply vanished, in which case he never divulged their final resting places. He would carefully fold his victim up in the trunk and drive him a couple hours west to the Delaware River Valley—if for no other reason than he found a nighttime drive in the country a strangely pleasant departure from Newark and the workaday whirl of contraband and extortion rackets.

And it was to just such pastoral scenery that Sid's mind turned ever more frequently in prison. As he strolled the yard, weaving between knots of cigarette-smoking convicts, Sid pondered his future. After all, he might not have been headed for the WPP but he sure as shinola couldn't return to Newark, much less his old line of work. Then again, with the remainder of his defense fund and triple that in sundry nest eggs, he could get by without a vocation. But Newark was all he knew—that and being a hood.

Sunny scenic tours of the Delaware Valley filled his daydreams, first as only something to mask the grim penitentiary life, then as the object of his post-prison life. Sid didn't really believe it could happen. After all, what would a guy like Sid do out there in the woods? Other than dump bodies, that is?

Magazines in prison can be hot commodities. Especially those with girls in them, the more skin the better. Or with guys in them, the more skin the better. But even though his fellow inmates respected him, Sid was low in the pecking order because he wasn't willing to jeopardize his early parole by pummeling his way up to Top Rooster. This meant that when the magazines came around he got *Highlights* and *Woodcraft Quarterly*. Well, there was also *Sports Astream* and maybe *Rod & Rifle*, but all references to and articles about guns and hunting had been edited out. And who wants to read about fish in the joint? After a few months of Goofus and Gallant, connect-the-dots, and centerfolds featuring "Wood Glues of the World," Sid picked up an outdoor magazine. It was nice to look at the pictures—they reminded him of the Delaware Valley. And sometimes there was an ad with a picture of a girl in red hiking boots. Better than nothing. Then there were the articles, which he began to read ever more avidly. A couple of issues later, the Deputy Warden found he had an appointment with a certain Mr. Bifulco.

Feet up on his desk, the D.W. carved at a fingernail with a shiv that had been stabbed in his side during a cafeteria melee two years before. Missed his kidney by a bologna rind. A gristly old guard ushered Sid into the office and stood him before the desk. As was his way, the D.W. didn't say anything for some minutes. He liked the cons to feel uncomfortable. That was his job, after all.

"Well, Bifulco," he finally drawled, adjusting his clip-on tie. "What can I do for you today?" Sarcasm, thick as peanut butter.

Sid spoke.

The D.W.'s feet hit the floor.

"A what?"

"A fishing rod."

The D.W. had a laugh like a spoon caught in the garbage disposal. But he brought it to an abrupt stop.

"All right, Bifulco: why?"

"I wanna learn how to fish." Sid shrugged.

"Bifulco, the only fish around here is on a bun with tartar sauce. What're you gonna fish for?"

"I wanna learn how, that's all, without the fish. I thought, y'know, I could learn to like cast an' stuff, like out on the athletic field."

"No way, Bifulco. Get outta here." The D.W. waved both hands at him like he was sending a bad meat loaf back to the cook. The guard put a hand on Bifulco's shoulder.

"Just thought I'd ask. I'm no troublemaker. I'm just in for my seven." Sid was already out the door.

But he didn't give up. A letter to the Warden diplomatically broached the subject. Shortly thereafter, the gristly guard appeared at his cell and croaked: "Time to see the Warden, Bifulco."

Sid soon found himself in the company of the

flashy blue sailfish and great red sockeye salmon flanking the Warden's oak-paneled office.

"By God, Bifulco, what kind of man asks for a fishing rod in a federal penitentiary?" Warden Lachfurst thundered. He was small and bald, with round spectacles that flashed like half-dollars.

Sid didn't know how to answer. He didn't get a chance to.

"I'll tell you what kind of man, dammit! An Outdoors Man, Bifulco. Is that what you are? An Outdoors Man?" Lachfurst fastened both fists to the desktop, leaned forward, and attempted to wither Sid with the heat of his scrutiny.

Sid folded his arms, raised his chin, and spoke forthrightly. "Well, Warden, you ask me, I'd say there's only one way to find out."

Taken aback by the cut of Sid's jib, Lachfurst came to attention, tapping a knuckle on the desktop.

Twenty-four days later, Sid had his rod.

At first the Warden just made a point of training the brass telescope perched in his office window on the athletic field. Then he happened by, gave Sid a few pointers. Then there was another office visit, a few fish stories, and then the fly rod and a how-to book. Then the fly-tying kit. And damned if Lachfurst didn't have Sid make up a bunch of salmon flies for the Warden's annual trip to Labrador.

Worm and bobber fishing didn't hook Sid "Sleep" Bifulco. It was the serious business of tackle fishing, of search and destroy. Catalogs filled with lures, lines, weapons, and gadgets. Magazines brimming with technique, exotic locales, and brash leaping fish. It all had a certain sense of fraternity, a sense of craft, hunt, and danger that Sid, a hood, enjoyed. Angling wasn't just about whacking fish, it was about the respect that came with being a whacker of fish. And it took hold of Sid as if angling was what he'd always been meant for, as if being a wiseguy was a soured career turn. Besides, he'd grown fond of red hiking boots.

Sid Bifulco—Izaak Walton reincarnate.

chapter **2**

Cryptobranchus alleganiensis is a salamander of grand proportions. It has a record length of twenty-nine inches and almost exclusively haunts rocky-bottomed segments of the Susquehanna River. By all reports, this muddy, girthsome, and deeply wrinkled beast is like some aquatic English bulldog, and twice as handsome. They call them hellbenders, and their apocryphal appearances in the Delaware River are favored upon a dot on the map labeled Hellbender Eddy, Pennsylvania. There hadn't been a sighting of one since 1888.

Just where the river stumbles down a set of rapids, a large, slowly swirling pool forms the famed Eddy. Pink Creek sneaks in at this bay, and a trail beside it connects the river bend to the town of Hellbender Eddy. It's a wee burg wedged between the river and the steep side of Little Hound Mountain, which is really more like a hill.

The better part of sixty minutes from any interstate, Hellbender Eddy is more than two and a half hours from New York City. It's situated on the winding, circuitous Route 241, across the river from New York. It has only one antique store and neither fresh bagels nor the Sunday *New York Times*. There are a few holiday cabins, mostly owned by Scranton businessmen. Downtown is comprised of a single restaurant—Chik's Five Star Diner—and little else.

It was a frosty May dawn, and the counter at Chik's was filled with locals. The joint was old, the walls painted a zillion coats of cream semigloss, its Formica counter stalwart, long, and black. White and black tiles made a checkerboard of the floor, and deco wall sconces gave the place a dull warm glow. A giant urn brewed coffee by the gallon, residual steam making the hashery mighty humid indeed. Two potted palms in the back thought they'd died and gone to heaven.

On weekdays, most of the locals drifted through Chik's for a container of coffee and a sauna.

Big Bob Stillwell and Little Bob Cropsey made their usual appearance on the way to the construction site where they worked.

"G'morning, fellahs." Chik smiled, his pencil-thin mustache curling devilishly. "Usual?"

Little Bob was poking around Big Bob's jump-suited girth with an old VHS camcorder he bought at a tag sale. "Yes, Chik, we will have the usual. Tell us what the usual is, Chik."

Chik looked into the lens, hesitating and smoothing his hair.

Big Bob lifted a meaty arm and looked down at Little Bob like something in his armpit stank.

"Must ya fool with that darn thing so early in the mornin'?" Big Bob let his arm drop and turned to Chik. "*Not* the usual. Just coffee and buttered rolls. Gotta cut out the fat." Big Bob punched himself in the gut.

"Chik, look into the camera. I want the usual. I don't got no weight problem." Chik smoothed his mustache and flashed a dirty smile at the camera. Then Little Bob saw Big Bob's unshaven face fill the view screen.

"I ain't got a 'weight problem.' I'm not talkin' about fat, I'm talkin' about cholesterol. Eggs and bacon is cholesterol, Bob. Cholesterol is bad for ya too. Don't ya even read the papers? Chik: coffee and rolls." Big Bob was a faithful reader of *Newstime* magazine and considered himself quite the scholar of current events. As a heavy equipment operator on major construction projects, there were plentiful lulls in the pile-driving that could be spent memorizing the news.

"Hey, Doc." Little Bob squirreled over to Lloyd Conti, who was farther down the counter. "Tell me about cholesterol, Doc. Into the camera." Video

Bob was also an equipment operator, but unlike Big Bob, his job kept him busy switching between backhoes and front loaders.

Lloyd swiveled on his stool, mopping his lips and Vandyke with a paper napkin. A pack of plastic-tipped cheroots peeked from a top pocket.

"Bob, I am not a doctor. I keep telling ya that. Just 'cause I do electrolysis doesn't mean I'm a doctor. And do ya think that if I were a doctor I'd be doin' small engine repair on the side? Don't ya think I'd be removing gallbladders or somethin'?" Lloyd turned back to his breakfast.

"Hey, Bob. Come 'ere, I'll tell ya about cholesterol!" Jenny Baker was down at the last stool, a cracked leather jacket draped over her shoulders and her blond hair pinned to the top of her head with a cocktail stirrer. A bit of a looker past her prime, Jenny drove a ten-wheel tanker for Red Eft Trout Farms. Everyone knew the routine: Chik liked to toy with her, get a little fresh, make her take a swing at him. It had become a game of sorts. He kept tally with a pencil on the side of the coffee urn.

"O.K., Jenny, tell us about cholesterol. Why is it bad for skinny people?" Little Bob stalked over to Jenny, zooming in and out on the beguiling smile she'd worked up for him.

"Lemme show ya. See this piece of toast? Ya focused your little camera on it?"

"Got it, Jenny. Now what?"

"Well, see how when I dip it in the egg yella?

That there, stuck to the end of my toast? Come in real close now."

"Got it, Jenny. Now what?"

"That's cholesterol."

"But why is it bad for skinny people? It don't make us fat."

"No it doesn't, Little Bob. But it ain't too good for their video cameras."

Bob's image of Jenny was suddenly smeared yolk yellow.

"Hey! Hey! Ya put egg yella on my lens!" Little Bob poked his camera around looking for a napkin. Gentle early morning chuckles rippled through the patrons. Little Bob felt a clamp on the back of his neck. It was Big Bob's meaty grasp.

"Must ya fool with that darn thing this early in the mornin'? C'mon, we got our stuff, now let's let these folks breakfast in peace." Big Bob led his stooped protégé out the door just as Russ Smonig slipped past them with a sleepy nod.

"How ya doin', Russ?" Chik was freshening coffees along the counter. "Heard you got into the shad real good last week. How many does that make it now?"

"Yeah, they're comin' up. Small bunches, all bucks." Russ was sandy-haired, with a prominent jaw, squinty eyes, and an edgy manner that betrayed the hardships of rural life. But strictly speaking, Russ wasn't a local. He hailed from Hartford, where he'd been an insurance executive. Pennsylvania became his roost about ten years before, after some domestic trouble, some said. These days he tried to make a go at being an outdoor writer while getting by tying flies and guiding. He lived in a two-tone sagging trailer on a quality slice of riverfront south of Hellbender Eddy. The land was his outright, his total net asset. He'd once had a five-year plan in which he became widely published, hosted a fishing show, and replaced his shack with a palatial log cabin. Now he didn't make plans beyond the next three weeks.

"But how many does that make it? What's your total?" Chik persisted. Huge numbers of shad entered the Delaware River each spring to spawn like salmon, and those who angled for them seriously kept score.

Russ looked a little uncomfortable, but divulged his tally.

"Seventy-five. Chik, just gimme a half-dozen sticky buns, two cups regular, and fill this thermos, O.K.?" Russ plunked his thermos on the Formica and pushed back on his stained fedora, trying not to look at the patrons along the counter as they rustled with awe.

"Seventy-five already, huh? Sure took a quick lead. Got a client this mornin', do you, Russ?" Chik queried from a cloud of steam at the urn.

"Yeah, I got a sport this morning." Russ's gaze wandered over the ceiling before he snatched a glance down the counter. The whole lot was giving him the envious, expectant eye.

"Well?" Russ looked back at them, and they

shifted, looking from one to the other. Jenny spoke up.

"C'mon, Russ. We want the shad report. Lot of us've been to all the usual spots—fish all day an' just pick up a handful. Where are ya takin' 'em? An' don't give us that doo-doo about 'trade secrets.' We ain't your sports. Not one of us can afford your guiding services. But we are your neighbors, and, well, the neighborly thing to do is tell us where you're takin' 'em, that's all. It's not like there's a shad shortage or anything, is there, Russ?"

The group grunted, nodding agreement.

Russ worked up a fatigued smile, the only kind he seemed capable of anymore. Living was hard and the rewards increasingly scarce. Either he was up at four a.m. and on the river with a sport jigging for walleye, burning the midnight oil tying up four hundred dry flies to fill an order, or he was huddled next to his kerosene heater laboring on yet another article that would be rejected by *Sports Astream* or *Bass Blaster*.

His transition from amateur to professional angler was complete: he caught a lot of fish and could land enough for three square meals at will. But it was all he could do to stay financially afloat, much less give away freebies to his neighbors.

"Tell you what, Jenny. Neighborly is as neighborly does. You throw some free trout into Ballard Pond for my supper, and I'll give you a river sweet spot. Lloyd, you give a tune-up on my Evinrude, and I'll point out where and how you just might get that Mr. Musky you're always talking about. And, Chik, you..."

"No charge, Mr. Smonig." Chik winked at Russ and pushed forward the thermos, plastic cups, and white bag crammed with sticky buns. Russ plucked the pen from behind Chik's ear, tore out a receipt from his pad, and started to draw a little map. Folks at the counter craned their necks to see. Russ kept lowering his shoulder to block their view.

"There you go, Chik. Walleye. See you use that size Rapala in that color, and troll it right along through those holes just as early in the morning as you can." Russ collected his stuff and turned sharply to the audience. "Good day, neighbors." He backed out the door.

Reverend Jim was waiting for him on the porch with one foot on the railing, his sharp red tongue poised in anticipation, and an ocher eye angled up at Russ. The Reverend's affection for Russ was genuine, but the emotional tie did not keep him from robbing Russ blind. He had been banished from the Smonig abode for stealing coins, and he would loot the truck's glove box at any opportunity. Russ walked past the Reverend, dipped his shoulder, and the crow hopped on, expressing joy with flicks of his tongue and fanning wings.

The Reverend Jim was named for a popular TV evangelist. As Russ climbed into his truck, the Reverend took his place on the International

Harvester's gearshift knob. He would hop down every time Russ shifted gears, then pop right back up. Turning the pickup's key for a while, Russ whispered curses at his reluctant ignition and eyed his black thieving friend.

Eating a piece of toast slathered in jam, Jenny sauntered out of the diner and over to the truck.

"Well, seeing as how you're at least willing to barter, might ya accept information? Hey, Reverend Jim—how's my baby?" Jenny waved at the bird, who uttered a low, curious rattle like dice in a cup.

Russ gave the key a rest. He dished up his fatigued smile for Jenny.

"O.K., Russ, just to show that I for one know how to be neighborly, I'll give ya the information free and see if your conscience doesn't do the rest. Ya have a new next-door neighbor." She chomped her toast, licking grape jam from her lips.

"At the Ballard place, I'll bet. I heard some cars over there. So?"

"Well, Russ honey, my brother Matt was over there turning on the water and gas and such. And do ya know what he saw?"

She arched an eyebrow. Russ's eyebrows remained the same.

"I'll tell ya what he saw. Your new next-door neighbor is not only from the city, but he is also loaded with fishing tackle. He's got rods sticking out all over the place. And in his pocket he keeps a wad of bills this thick. Tipped Matt ten bucks, just like that." Jenny shoved the rest of the toast in her mouth.

"Might not need any guiding if he has all that tackle." Russ's lips puckered in thought.

"Russ, don't be a dope," she said around the toast, swallowing hard. "It don't matter how many rods he got. He's not from around here! He doesn't know the hot spots like you do, now does he?"

Russ's eyebrows arched. Reverend Jim began clucking impatiently.

"Let's put it this way, Smonig: if you do get this new neighbor as a sport, I want a little map like you gave Chik, but with an X marking the secret shad spot." Jenny licked jam from her thumb.

Russ looked up at her sharply.

"It's a deal." He cranked the key and seemed to catch the ignition off guard. The truck started.

Like most crows, Reverend Jim was clever to the verge of being psychic. He never failed to show up when Russ was headed for Phennel Rowe's place, and as it happened Russ planned to drop off some fish fillets there on his way back from the Five Star.

"I hears you got a new neighba', Mr. Smonig," Phennel croaked from her gray porch rocker. A hand-painted black and olive sign hung low over the porch steps: "ANTIQUES—Used Furniture." A similar sign posted like a warning in the yard declared "LAMPERS," which referred to the baby blood-sucking eels that Phennel dug out of the mucky bends in Pink Creek. Lampers were hot commodities, especially when she came into a bevy of blue lampers, considered the hottest summer walleye bait at any price.

"So I hear." The Reverend fidgeted on Russ's forearm as they approached the sagging Victorian house.

"And Reverend Jim is come too. Why, do ya remember the first time ya brought that bird 'roun' here? That was a sorry sight." Phennel shook her head, rocked a moment, then stopped and put bent, oversized spectacles on her face.

"Yup." Russ paused at the porch steps. "Found him with a mangled foot, brought him to you, and you fixed him up." The crow was left with one good foot and one stump, and when he walked he limped like a peg-leg pirate.

"Ya mean the Reverend Jim Chattanooga fixed him up. I only doctored him. It was the five dollars I sent to Reverend Jim for a TV prayer that put the Lord's healing in that bird. What ya got there, Mr. Smonig?" She knew, or should have known. He brought fillets every week. Maybe she didn't want it to seem like charity.

"Shad and walleye. I had extra and thought maybe you could use some. Only seems right, what with you paying that five dollars for that prayer." Russ ducked under the hanging sign and stepped up onto the porch. As he did so, the crow hopped onto Phennel's shoulder and cawed in her bad ear.

"Why, that's very thoughtful, Mr. Smonig. No roe yet, I suppose?" She looked up at him through her glasses, her wet sloe eyes searching his. Phennel was a sensitive, spiritual woman, and she could see pain in a person's eyes.

"No, not yet. I'll just put these in your icebox." Russ made his way through the flimsy screen door, and Phennel nodded her thanks. He returned shortly, conscious both of the sport waiting at his trailer and of Phennel's probing eyes. He tipped his hat, ready to mumble his good-bye. Miss Rowe interrupted.

"Ya missin' Sandra pretty bad lately? If ya like, Russell, come by this evening for some Postum, and we'll talk."

The name Sandra stung. Russ nodded at the offer of instant mock coffee, smiled weakly, and moved off to his truck without a word.

When he climbed in, he discovered that the Reverend had jimmied the glove box and flown off with his Pabst bottle opener.

chapter
3

Sid arose to the distant applause of the river and wandered into his knotty pine kitchen. In a dented saucepan he whipped up some instant coffee. Steaming mug in hand, he shuffled through the tackle-strewn living room and kicked open the door to the porch. Squirrels exploded out of the rafters and dove for a gnaw hole in the porch screen. They were gone. Sid casually examined the leafy nest they'd fled as he settled into a PVC lawn chair.

The weather had been unsettled, overcast skies spotted with teasing peeks of blue and the stray ray of sun. It was frosty out and early in the season for any frog or insect to make much racket in the morning. Only the river, which was running a little high, kicked up a fuss. All in all it was about as quiet as it got at Ballard Cabin, which was just about perfect musical accompaniment for Sid's first morning alone in seven years. Piquant and piney country air filled his nose, an aroma he hoped would soon vanquish the lingering whiff of prison stench.

Everything had happened just as he'd mapped it out over the years. His lawyer, Endelpo, had hatched Sid's various nest eggs, sent him real estate clippings, cinched the deal on the cabin, and gotten him an LTD to replace his long-gone Marquis. Acknowledging that keeping Sid in New Jersey during probation might be a death sentence, Warden Lachfurst had been instrumental in negotiating a parole that allowed Sid to relocate. Of course he had to keep in close contact with his probation officer, a man who by no coincidence was a "bronze back" enthusiast. His P.O. had accompanied him to his new digs, and after inspecting the river advised Sid that he didn't really expect him to seek employment so much as find him the smallmouth bass. No need for Sid to visit him in Newark. He would be back often enough, rod in hand. As would, in time, Warden Lachfurst. And maybe one or two trout-mad members of the parole board.

So in effect, Sid had cut a deal with the prosecutors for a short sentence, with the Camuchis for eliminating anybody who would possibly come after him, and with the anglers on the parole board for the ability to relocate to a fishing outpost.

Ballard Cabin was a simple affair—bedroom, living room, kitchen, and screened porch facing toward the river, out over an embankment. The outside was shingled and painted brown, with forest green trim. The inside was knotty pine adorned with paint-by-number oils, numerous floor lamps, and two resident examples of taxidermy—a pickerel and a deer head that tendered the eerily ingratiating leer of the Great Bear Transmission logo. The cabin was nestled under a stand of white pine, and from the embankment at the back porch, overgrown grass and saplings cluttered the sweep down to a stony shoal and light rapids. Abutments from a washed-out bridge stood on each shore just downstream.

Sid sucked in the piney air and exhaled the prison stench. Now and again he took a sip of coffee as he admired the peaceful surroundings. But it wasn't long before he heard a truck drive up the road and turn down his neighbor's drive.

An Eldorado with a "Semper Fi" bumper sticker was waiting for Russ when he returned to his trailer. Russ marshaled his cheeriest demeanor and pulled up next to his visitor.

"How-do. I'm Russ Smonig. Ready to try for some shad?"

Russ hopped out of his truck toting the white breakfast bag. The iguana-like man leaning on the Eldorado stepped forward.

"I should say so! Been here twenty minutes. Was about ready to bug out. Don't know why you had roll call so damned early if I was just going to come stand by this shed. And what's this about *trying* for shad? By golly, Smonig, if you can get shad for that partner of mine, you'll get shad for me."

Russ just kept smiling. "Now that's the spirit! Well, we're wasting time. The boat's all loaded, down by the river."

The Iguana croaked, pushing up his sleeves. "Now hold it, Smonig. Seventy-five bucks for a half day, right?"

"That's right."

"From the time we hit the water, I assume?"

"O.K., yes, that's right." The cheery smile was withering.

"Well, let's get this thing organized first, d'ya mind? I got rods here an' I need to know which weapon to take. And ammo—I've got salmon flies. But if I run outta bullets I expect you to resupply me at no extra cost."

"Excuse me." Russ blinked. "You want to fly-fish for shad? It's really a little early in the season for that. The water's high. You'd need a full sink line and..."

"Smonig, you shoulda told me that over the phone...."

"Well, when your partner was here we used spinning tackle. I assumed you wanted to do the same."

"Smonig, I never, ever, use spinning tackle."

* * *

A squirrel small enough to fit in a coffee cup ventured forth from the nest in the porch rafters and spied on Sid for some time before drawing near.

Sid sipped his instant coffee, viewed the river, and kept an eye on the inquisitive young squirrel. At the same time he monitored the tone of garbled conversation from his next-door neighbor's, which was out of view beyond a stand of tall weeds, a service-berry hedge, some bulrushes, and a lopsided willow. Fly reels whizzed and clattered, doors creaked and slammed, two men conversed in earnest. At long last the activity subsided.

As Sid tried to figure where the activity had gone, he felt a tentative twitching on the shoulder of his bathrobe. Whiskers brushed his graying side-burn and a rapid wuffling filled his ear. The pup squirrel was searching his ear for pine nuts.

Years of wariness, both in prison and the Newark rackets, had trained Sid to react slowly but no less definitively to prodding, whether the stimulus be the barrel of a 9 mm, a shiv, or a baby squirrel. He turned his head slowly toward the wee rodent, who grasped at his lobe in a vain effort to keep the ear from drifting away. But he was diverted by Sid's stare. The squirrel's huge black pupils stared back. He sniffed for a moment, put both forepaws on Sid's nose, and began to look up his nostrils.

"Cute lil' mother." Sid chuckled, just before two yellow incisors clamped on his nostril flange.

A zap of pain shot Sid to his feet. The pup squir-rel vaulted for the rafters, where he chattered a warning from the confines of the leafy nest.

Sid held his nose, checked his fingers for blood, and looked up.

"You'n me have to have a little talk sometime." He squinted at the squirrel's nest. But the gurgling snare of a distant outboard motor snatched his at-tention.

Clawing through the pile of gear in the living room, Sid came up with trout-spotting binoculars and charged out the front door just as fast as his bedroom slippers would take him. With the agility of a kid scaling a fence, he hopped onto the por-tico's wood rail, got a leg up onto the roof of the cabin, and scrambled on all fours to the limb of a white pine. Making his way along the limb to the trunk, Sid drew his red satin robe against the ele-ments, tightened his sash, and trained the binocu-lars on a boat motoring down the rapids.

The well-placed mole on Sid's cheek vanished in the grin that worked up one side of his face, a row of even wrinkles blending into his nicely pleated crow's-feet.

A guy in a brown fedora stood at the stern working the boat backward through the rapids with practiced skill. Another guy stood in the bow waving his arms and pointing at the river.

The outboard was silenced. On the river's far side, Captain Fedora draped a claw anchor over the side and fed it rope. Line taut, the boat swung around smartly in the heavy current, putting the bow downstream. In what appeared to be a demonstration for a pupil, Captain Fedora stood and began false casting in luxurious brown loops that finally unfurled his fly forward and across the current. After letting it drift down current, he reeled up and sat back down.

The pupil stood and prepared by slowly pulling line from his reel and looping it neatly in one hand. Captain Fedora cringed as his pupil's fly zipped closer and closer to his head. But he didn't interrupt Pupil, who finally let loose a noodly cross-stream cast. This was repeated for about twenty minutes. Nothing. Pupil started pointing fingers at Captain Fedora just as the latter weighed anchor and moved the boat fifteen feet farther downstream.

Pupil shrugged and looked as if he wished he could hail a cab. But after some fussing and finger-pointing, he got another cast out.

When his line snapped taut from the water, Pupil stumbled in surprise. Captain Fedora grabbed him by the jacket to steady him.

Silver arced like a shard of glass from the water in a high, shimmering leap of fish. Pupil fumbled, then reeled up his slack line. The fish was gone.

"Whoa." Sid tugged thoughtfully at his ear. Except for a flounder outing off Sea Girt, New Jersey, Sid had never seen a fish caught, much less jump. His buddies referred to fluke as "doormats" for obvious reasons. Sid had dragged in his share of doormats that day, and some had fallen off the hook too. But here was a jumping, rocketlike fish—whatever it was—and it had gotten away.

"Huh," Sid muttered, bolstering his morale. "That rocket-fish had been my fish? It'd be in the boat." Sid's own bravado made him a little uncomfortable. As he adjusted his footing, he noticed something twinkling in the deep crease where the branch and trunk met. Crouching, he brushed away some needles, uncovering a handful of coins, jigs, paper clips, keys, buttons, and a Pabst bottle opener. He stood, shrugged off his mild curiosity, and retrained his binoculars on the river.

An hour went by as the pupil hooked and lost one rocket-fish after the other. As soon as a fish was hooked, it blasted about thirty feet upstream and launched right out of the water, throwing the lure. Captain Fedora tried to make a few suggestions, but apparently Pupil didn't care to be taught.

Eventually, a fish was soundly hooked, played, netted, and boated. Pupil sat down and pointed toward shore. Captain Fedora shrugged and hauled up the anchor. The boat wended neatly through the rapids and disappeared from Sid's view. And high time. His shoulders and feet were worse for wear from the rough pine bark. Sid's carpet slippers and satin bathrobe weren't exactly lumberjack gear.

He was startled by the sigh of air brakes behind him. He turned to see the Red Eft Trout Farms truck lumbering down his driveway.

"Hey, neighbor. What ya doin' up in that tree in

your bathrobe?" A woman hollered from the cab as she brought the truck to a stop in front of Ballard Cabin. She jumped down from the cab. "Ya didn't sleep up there, did ya? What are ya? An airline pilot? Ya like sleepin' as close to the clouds as possible?"

Sid blinked and set his jaw. She was wearing crimson hiking boots.

"Yeah? And who the fuck are you?"

"Nice mouth, neighbor!" She jerked a thumb back at the tanker truck and snapped her bubble gum. "Red Eft Trout Farms. I'm Jenny. Here to stock your pond."

"I don't got no pond." With the confidence of an alley cat, Sid made his way from the limb to the roof and made for the portico.

"Sure ya do. What, didn't them real estate folks show ya the pond? Nobody told ya 'bout the pond?" Jenny walked up to the portico where Sid was brushing pine needles from his robe. He found them sticking to his fingers. Sap.

"O.K., so if there's a pond, where is it?" He gestured broadly to his front yard, then rubbed his hands together to shoo away the pine needles. He only succeeded in rearranging them.

Five minutes later, Sid was still in his bathrobe but sporting hip boots. Rubbing a paper towel over the sap on his fingers, he followed Jenny into the tall weeds and serviceberry thicket. A few paces in, Jenny stopped.

"See? Now, do ya want trout in it or not?"

Weeds and hedge, left unchecked, had conspired to obscure the long, narrow pond from view. A rapidly flowing, skinny creek merrily winding its way to the Delaware met an elfin earthen dam at the edge of the embankment. Outflow coursed through a pipe embedded in the dam, which doubled as a bridge. Sid estimated Ballard Pond to be four times the size of a bocci ball court.

The prospect of owning a pond thrilled Sid almost as much as the prospect of Jenny's red hikers, but you wouldn't have known it to look at him.

"You call that a pond?" He finally balled up the tattered paper towel and stuffed it in his robe pocket, his hands flecked with paper towel.

"The Ballards did. And every year they had the farm come out and chuck in fifty twelve-inch brook trout. So whaddaya say, sport? Want your own lil' trout pond?"

"Could be there's still some trout left from last year."

"Don't think so, sport. Ballard died last spring, just after stocking. Kids were in all last summer catching 'em any way they could." Jenny pushed past Sid, making for her truck.

She just had the truck door open when she heard: "How much?"

Jenny turned and handed him the pink invoice. Sid produced a wad of bills from his bathrobe pocket.

* * *

"Damn, Smonig—that was some real frontline fishing. How much you think this roe shad weighs?" The Iguana was tromping in Russ's wake through the high grass and toward the trailer. Hanging from his stringer was a shad that looked like a large startled herring.

"Four, maybe going on five," Russ lied. "Definitely the best one you had on." Roe shad were commonly four to six pounds; buck shad rarely broke four pounds. The bloody critter the sport had bagged was just a bit better than three.

The Iguana was quite pleased with his trophy, though, and when they reached the car and he had all his stuff packed up, he handed Russ the borrowed reel along with the seventy-five-dollar fee. And that was that. For a sport so well pleased, a tip is usual, but Russ was just glad they didn't haggle over the fact that they'd only been on the water two and a half hours, even though it was the Iguana who insisted they head in after he had his fish.

As soon as the Eldorado and "Semper Fi" disappeared up the drive, Russ stopped waving bye-bye and turned toward his trailer. It was Friday, Russ had his seventy-five bucks, and before you knew it, it would be Saturday night, when he would head over to the Duck Pond Bar for a beery respite. In the meantime, Russ's choice of activities included finishing an article for *Fly-Fishing Gazette*, a complimentary tackle store rag for which he was compensated with a free three-line ad for his guiding services. Or he could tie a bunch of early season flies for the local tackle shop, a labor-intensive undertaking that netted him a whopping five dollars an hour. Or he could attempt to exorcise the demon from the International's ignition, potentially making money by avoiding giving it to the mechanic.

A truck's backup beep sounded from behind the willow. The crunch of weeds and the snap of twigs followed. The seventy-five dollars tucked in his back pocket, Russ decided to see what was up on the other side of the hedge. He veered from the trailer, went past the barbecue pit, and came to a stop next to the willow at the edge of Ballard Pond.

The serviceberry bushes parted, tiny white petals from their flowers snowing onto the red satin bathrobe of the guy in hip boots coming into view. Beyond him, red round taillights approached.

"Hold it," Sid barked, and the taillights went bright. The back tires of the truck were beginning to make ruts in the mud. The beeper stopped, the air brakes sneezed. Jenny came around the other side of the truck.

"Yeah, that's close enough." Jenny disappeared for a second, then reappeared with a long-handled net. She scaled a ladder on the back of the truck to the top, where she opened a tank lid.

"O.K., sport, here's how we'll count 'em. I pull up a net full—usually five fish—then I say 'five,' hold it down for ya to check, then chuck the fish into the pond, O.K.?"

"Let's get somethin' straight, you an' me. I'm no sport. You call me Sid, got it? Second, you're not chucking anything. There's a bucket on the side of the truck. I fill it with water, you *place* my fish in the bucket of water, and I will put my fish *gently* into the pond. Got it?"

Jenny grinned. "Whatever ya say, sport. Uh, Sid. And ya can just keep calling me 'lady,' thank ya very much." She already had the net down in the tank. Sid grabbed the bucket and filled it with water from the pond.

On the first attempt, two fish catapulted out of the pail into the leafy underbrush, from whence Sid had to nudge the leaf-matted critters with his foot to the very edge of the pond. By the time they made it to the water they looked like squirming cigars.

So Sid filled the next bucket only halfway, and there were no more escapes. Somewhere around the fifth bucket, he spied his Captain Fedora watching from the far bank, though he paid him little attention. Fifteen minutes later, all fifty trout were gently delivered and the truck was pulling out of the bushes. Sid took a last look and saw his neighbor was gone. However, when he got back to his driveway he found the guy exchanging a few words with Trout Lady.

Sid walked between them and handed a twenty up to Jenny in the truck. "Here. Make sure you don't tell nobody about my trout. I wanna keep the locals outta my pond. Got it?"

Jenny snapped the bill taut, put it in her teeth,

and wrestled the truck into gear. Through her teeth she said: "Neighbor, ya got a deal!" She pulled away, looking in the rearview mirror.

Sid pulled an about-face.

His neighbor put out one hand and jerked the thumb of the other back at the pond.

"Nice to see you're stocking the pond. Hi, I'm Russ Smonig, your neighbor."

As was his way, Sid considered the extended hand a moment before clasping it. Shaking hands, he stared into Captain Fedora's eyes. Then his other hand swooped up and latched onto Russ's shoulder.

"Sponick?" Sid asked.

"No, Smonig. Russ Smonig."

"Sid." Sid gestured casually to himself. "Hey, Smonig, you know anything about kids comin' in here swiping trout?"

"Sure. Hard to stop 'em though. It's just the way kids are, you know?"

"Hm." Sid supposed that was true enough. It seemed his entire childhood had revolved around swiping things, though certainly not trout. "These kids, do they, like, climb up that tree? That one, the sticky one over my house."

"Um, I don't know, Sid. Why?"

"Just curious. There's a bottle opener up there, and a buncha loose change."

"Up in the tree? Up there? Where?" Russ took a sudden interest.

"Why, you know who put it up there?"

"It must be Reverend Jim. He's been stealing stuff from me for years and I never knew what he did with—"

"Whoa. You tellin' me that your local padre climbs up that tree and puts your pocket change up there?" These yokels were a pisser.

"Reverend Jim is a crow. You know, a bird. Kind of like a pet, sort of. He likes to steal shiny objects. Was it a Pabst opener?"

Sid's eyes widened. "I think so."

"Mind if I go up and..."

"Sure, Smonig, g'head, knock yourself out." Sid shooed Russ toward the porch as though it were a gag. Why would anybody climb all the way up there for a bottle opener?

Russ had a dicey moment making it onto the roof from the portico railing, but did it without falling. Minutes later he was back on the ground, breathing hard.

"I even found the keys to my padlock. I thought I'd just lost them. And there must be, let's see, maybe three bucks in change. This is great," he panted.

Sid wondered if everybody in Hellbender Eddy was so hard up.

"Uh, you move here with your wife?" Russ asked as he pocketed his goodies.

Sid shook his head.

"Nope. Just me." He gave Russ's shoulder a quick squeeze and pulled him a step closer. "Tell you what, Smonig. Whenever you see kids here, chase 'em off, wouldya? I'll let you fish the pond all you want—catch an' release, of course. I'll even give you a brand-new bottle opener. Deal?"

"Catch and release? I don't expect I'll fish the pond, you know, what with a whole river out there. Besides, the Ballards pretty much used it as an eatin'-fish pond, if you know what I mean. Fed 'em strips of bacon fat and salt pork. Made 'em tasty as all get out."

Sid gave Russ's shoulder another squeeze. "The Ballards is dead." The remark was framed with a cold, bright eye and a chummy smile. He wanted Smonig to understand that from now on it was Bifulco Cabin. He let his hand fall from Russ's shoulder.

"True enough," Russ admitted, becoming a bit skeptical of the prospects for selling his services as Jenny had suggested. His neighbor was a tough customer. But he forged ahead.

"Hey, Sid, since you just moved in and all, and maybe you haven't got around to doing any food shopping, I thought maybe you'd like to come over tonight. I'm going to barbecue some walleye, have a few Yuenglings. Interested?"

Sid grinned.

"Thanks, but I got a lot to do." Sid shoved his hands into the pockets of his bathrobe and stomped in his hip boots back to the cabin. "Adios, Smonig."

"Hey, Sid?"

Sid stopped on his portico and pivoted.

"Nice outfit." Russ smiled and turned away. He was crossing the dam breast when he heard Sid's screen door slam.

Russ shook his head. Some neighbor.

chapter **4**

Late that afternoon, Sid was loaded for bear. His vest was packed with fly boxes, leaders, floatants, extra spools, clippers, snippers, hemostats, thermometer, and license. Two fly rods—one sturdy bass-weight rod and the more delicate trouter's rod—plus a medium-duty spin cast outfit. Hip boots, jumpsuit, long-brimmed ball cap, and polarized shades. Off went Sid, down an overgrown path, headed for the Ballard boat and his angling destiny.

The Ballard rowboat was next to the old bridge abutment. It was speckled gray aluminum, lying upside down, with one end propped up on a stump. When Sid flipped it over, two barn swallows bolted from a nest built under one of the seats. Sid chiseled the clay bird's nest off with a stick. The oars were wedged under the seats, but he left them where they were while he dragged the boat down the embankment and fifty feet over to a small bay. By the time both tackle and Sid were aboard and the oars were in the locks, he was breaking a sweat as much from the anticipation as from the exertion.

Sid studied the rapids. From a river-level vantage, it was difficult to see the spot where Smonig had set up, but he knew it was on the other side, and that didn't look too easy to get to. Sure, if he had a motor, getting there wouldn't be a problem. Sid wiggled the oars in the air and checked out his biceps. He was a strong guy, he'd worked out regularly in the prison gym.

And an even, warm breeze was blowing downriver.

Russ was on his way to pull his boat out of the river before it rained. Halfway there, he saw Sid below the rapids in a rowboat, oars hacking away at the water in great splashes like a clipped-wing swan attempting flight. He was struggling upriver against a heavy current.

Russ quickened his step, and when he reached his boat, he fetched his binoculars.

Mid-rapid and rowing ferociously, Sid suddenly dropped the oars, grabbed the anchor, and tossed it overboard. The anchor didn't hold, and the boat was washed down out of the rapid. So Sid hauled in the anchor, put it on the seat next to him, and pulled the swan routine again until he was in heavy current. And again the anchor didn't hold.

Lowering the binoculars, Russ faced upstream, took off his fedora, and let the warm, moist air play with his sandy hair. He could tell just from the texture of the breeze that it was already raining up in Hancock, so he went about his business. By the time he had the boat out of the river and covered up, the first raindrops were thwacking the tarp. Squinting across the river, he noted that Sid was finally set up in the current and casting a fly. Russ shrugged and headed for the shelter of his trailer.

No sooner had he sat down at the ol' computer to finish his article "Best Bet for Browns" than there was the hesitant flash, crack, and boom of lightning overhead. The sky opened up, and soon drops from the ceiling plunked into the Folgers can on the kitchen floor.

Muddy swells boiled around Sid's bucking rowboat and he was ankle deep in water. But it was the lightning that convinced him this was no passing shower. Time to abort his mission.

Rain fell steadily. Deep below, the scrap-iron anchor was wedged in a rocky fissure. Despite Sid's rebukes it wouldn't budge, and he realized he'd soon be swamped or pulled under the rising river. The one tool he didn't have was a knife, so he clawed at the frayed rope's tight, wet knot fastened to the bow. Meanwhile, there was commotion astern—the fly line and fly he'd left drifting in the current jerked taut. Fish on. The rod clattered toward the edge of the boat. Sid lunged. And missed. The rod disappeared into the river chop, but not before Sid grabbed a loop of line caught on an oarlock.

The sky split with light, there was a heartbeat, then a profound discharge that Sid felt in his fillings. He reared to his feet, pier after pier of rain swirling round him as he began to haul up the line.

An electric spear shattered the dark, swirling sky, and the flashing blade of a rocket-fish broke the surface downstream. A hooked shad played tug-o-war with Sid's one hand while the other hand felt the distant rattle of line peeling from his fly reel, deep in the weedy bay below.

Turbid river water began to top the gunnels; Sid realized the river had him by the balls. That's when the anchor rope snapped, and the jolt shoved Sid backward. He staggered as the boat swung suddenly around. Man overboard.

The sky splintered with light, but Sid couldn't hear the storm's explosions. Fly line was tangled around his legs, and whitecaps kicked his head against the twirling aluminum hull. He clung to a gunnel by elbow and armpit—to let go would be to join guys that got popped. Boulders nudged him from below. And all the while, he could still feel a well-hooked rocket-fish tugging at one end of the line, like it was sewing him up in a body bag.

*   *   *

It was almost nine that evening by the time the rain stalled, but Russ had the barbecue pit stoked even as the clouds were running out of gas. Fillets steeped in garlic and beer, topped with strips of bacon, hissed and browned over the coals. Russ sat in a sagging Adirondack chair, one foot on the edge of the brick oven, one hand around a cold Yuengling beer. The other hand held a blue plastic water pistol ready to put out any bacon fires. Eyes alight with the fire, his thoughts turned to Sandra.

Perhaps the most debilitating aspect of his past tragedy was the emotional baggage he'd packed for himself. At the bottom of this steamer trunk of pain was self-loathing over his inability to prevent Sandra's death.

On top of that was his frustration over trying to prove or convince the police that his wife's "accident" had been murder. Russ had truly hit rock bottom when his friends and family began scolding him for his assertions. They felt he was dragging Sandra's name through the mud, that he was indirectly suggesting she must have been involved with criminals to be the target of murder. They took to psychoanalyzing him, telling him he was flipped-out from despair, or suffering effects from the bump on his head, or concocting a cover-up for some misdeed on his part.

Near the top of the trunk rested the conundrum of why someone had killed her in the first place, a question with which police, friends, and family pelted him and for which he had no answer.

It had been ten years since her death, and the sickly sweet taste of regret had become familiar enough that it was not altogether overwhelming. Over the last couple of years he'd been able to set that aside and remember Sandra herself, the woman he loved, and the time they'd had together, however brief.

He smiled at the thought of their first meeting, when they'd scraped fenders at Bradley Airport parking lot and subsequently found themselves seated on the same flight, side by side. Their relationship warmed over dinner and the next few months. Eventually, she took him to small claims court over the traffic accident, and when she won, she used the money to take him to Montego Bay for a week, where they got married to the accompaniment of a steel drum calypso band. Russ burned the photos from that trip after Sandra died. The evidence of his loss was too damn painful to have around. Of course, destroying all those photos was just one more thing to regret, one more garment in the trunk. But he'd managed to rescue one photo of their honeymoon, which she'd kept at her office. It hung over Russ's fly-tying desk, and sometimes when he saw it, he felt a little like smiling. Those were the good days.

Russ had decided against Postum with Phennel Rowe. Although she never tired of hearing of his pain, Russ did. After a while, it all seemed perverse, masochistic. He was sick of hearing his own voice, his own sighs, and his own doubts. Phennel's languid creaky words of comfort and religion were like ice on a burn. It didn't really help, it only made the boo-boo feel better for a while. Russ never much liked himself after those sessions. He had determined to try going it alone. Alone with that picture.

So on this night, rather than wallowing in self-pity, he was taking a dip in the warm bittersweet waters of the tragic true romance of his past.

But he was snapped from his trance by a ghoulish apparition near the willow tree.

Russ spasmed with fright, toppling his chair. He fell backward, Yuengling gushing all over his chest. Scrambling away from the demon stomping up from the pond, Russ slipped on the wet grass in a frenzied lurch, did a half twist, and fell on his butt facing The Creature.

Panic melted away, along with all his blood. Russ almost fainted before he realized what he was looking at.

The Creature stopped abreast of the barbecue pit, clothes torn and muddy, blood running from its nose, and hair in matted tussocks with twigs for accents. Fly line wrapped like mummy tape around its shoulders and legs. One hand held up a battered fish, its silvery moon-eyed countenance held forth like the bizarre lantern of a sea witch. His neighbor's flame-flickered visage gurgled, then spoke.

"Smonig, what...is...this...thing?"

Russ got to his feet, wanting to curse and ask a

question at the same time. Instead, he heard himself stammer: "It's . . . it's a shad."

Sid nodded blankly, turned, and tromped back into the forest shadows, disappearing behind the willow from whence he'd come.

chapter **5**

Endelpo Thuarte, attorney-at-law, had just re-turned to New Jersey from a late-season ski trip to Vail. And no sooner had he loaded up his gear and strapped his skis on the ol' BMW than he was tool-ing across the Pulaski Skyway toward his Hoboken brownstone, popping vitamins and hitting the speed-dial on his cellular to canvass for a late-night sup with a lady friend.

After leaving several messages, the phone rang back at him. But there was nobody on the other end. Endelpo thought nothing of it. He continued his search for a date.

Mr. Thuarte was a man who lived by a golden rule: work hard, play hard, keep your nose clean. Translated, this meant carry the heaviest caseload, get laid as often as possible, don't double-cross anybody. His forte was defending small-time mobsters, and for all intents and purposes he was on the Camuchi syndicate's payroll, the very same outfit that had cut Sid Bifulco the sweet deal. All in all Endelpo was a pretty dandy fellow, unless of course you happened to get pregnant. Even then he was quick to offer to pay for an abortion.

The tan BMW growled down the gaslit and sycamore-lined lane and turned into his driveway; he poked at the automatic garage door opener but nothing happened. Repeated jabs at the button yielded no better results. He unclipped the gizmo from the visor. His white Italian loafers took his ski-jacketed form right up to the garage door, where Endelpo fired the zapper point blank. The door capitulated. It began to rise.

But the light didn't snap on.

"Jesus! It's always somet'ing, this door." Endelpo returned to his car.

The garage was empty except for an old Jacuzzi resting on its side. He pulled the car right up to the whirlpool and switched off the headlights and engine.

The garage door closed automatically, shutting out what little light the streetlamps had cast. By the glow of the BMW's dome light, Endelpo made his way to the wall switch. He flipped it up. He flipped it down. He waggled it. Then he squinted in the direction of the bulb. It was broken, smashed.

Endelpo went rigid. The house key in his hand burned. Could he get it in the lock, quickly?

Turning toward the door, he saw a large human shape emerge from behind the Jacuzzi. Endelpo's ears rang, his gut went soggy. The ominous shape moved toward him. The keys that had been in Endelpo's fingers hit the garage floor. Large hands cut into the wedge of glow from the dome light. Endelpo couldn't take his eyes off the hands, especially when the digits laced and the knuckles popped.

"Where's Bifulco?" a chilly, empty voice asked.

Mr. Phillips was at home in his cozy New York brownstone on Grove Street, the kind embellished with an elaborate wrought-iron fence, rails, and window guards. Surrounded by his collection of historically significant shell casings neatly arrayed in lighted wall displays, he was considering a prized .30 caliber brass casing fired on a sunny November day in 1963. A former Texas politician had given it to Mr. Phillips for his services during a reelection campaign.

Those were the days. But now he was older, wiser, so he thought, and content to work small-time and relatively safe jobs for the Camuchi family. Officially, he was retired.

Omer Phillips was no hit man, and he certainly didn't look like one. He was a slight, dark man with somewhat pointy ears and high cheekbones. A chess prodigy as a boy, young Omer's aptitude was incongruous with his Turkish family's Coney Island homestead. But when any of his eight older brothers got pinched by the cops, they came to their little brother Omer for a way out. And he usually found one, or got beat up. By his teens, Omer had dropped formal chess competitions for speed matches on the boardwalk and the quick buck. And when he sought a trade in the sideshows, he shunned his family's sword stunts for an apprenticeship with Dr. Renaldo, the hypnotist and noted gangland spy. It was said Omer had once put the chief of police in a trance from an adjoining toilet stall.

Omer's talents took him far from Coney Island's sideshows. In his adult heyday, of course, Omer worked for politicians, anything from covering up a boozy nocturnal tryst-cum-car-crash to banishing the ex-girlfriends of presidential hopefuls. However, his tours de force were "arrangements" whereby a third party got trigger-happy and someone notable died. This had the benefit of adding to his immense collection of infamous shell casings. But the whole scene got too frantic after Watergate. He still got calls from the Washington crowd but did fewer and fewer well-paying "favors" like the one for Ollie. Bill's mess was ample evidence of the void left by Omer. Omer was not an assassin. Obstructer of justice? Definitely. Tamperer of evidence? Most assuredly. Briber, extortionist, conspirator, and manipulator? All of the above.

Nowadays, Omer's work was simple, just the way

he liked it. Some Johnny Dangerous has a pissed-off girlfriend threatening to talk to Mrs. Dangerous, the press, the cops—anybody to get back at Johnny? Enter Mr. Phillips. Perhaps said girlfriend would have some kind of outstanding warrant for prostitution in Atlantic City. Or maybe delinquent tax returns. Even an old beau with a vicious bent. Possibly all three. All it usually took was a little fatherly advice and a dab of homespun extortion. Often a smattering of hypnotic suggestion was helpful.

When the call came in at ten p.m., Omer leisurely answered on the seventh ring.

"I'm very sorry, Monseigneur, I got thuh wrong numba." The caller hung up.

Omer buttoned his plaid vest, straightened his bow tie in the mirror, plopped his gray woolen crusher atop his silver hair, and slipped an umbrella out of the stand on the way out the door.

Once in his blue Karmann Ghia and out of the garage, he motored down Broadway and stopped at a Worth Street pay phone. He dialed a number.

A murky, mortuary voice answered.

"O.K., Mr. Phillips, you got a job."

"Always here to help. It must be serious, at this hour." Omer twirled his umbrella.

"I'd say so, Mr. Phillips, I'd say so. Johnny Fest is escaped from thuh Newark overnight lockup infirmary for stomach pains. Was due in court. Killed a guard. Pushed his eyes into his brain. Stole some clothes from hospital staff, a candy-stripers' shirt. On thuh loose. We want to make sure thuh cops find him. Quick, like before he whacks anybody, friends, lawyers... You know what I'm talkin' about?"

"Yes, I've got you covered. I'll let you know tomorrow. Good-bye." Omer hung up and stared at the phone, rapidly tapping the steel tip of his umbrella on the sidewalk.

He popped a quarter, called information, and got the nice operator to give him Endelpo Thuarte's address.

Endelpo still wore his ski jacket. He lay facedown but at the same time faceup on the kitchen floor. To be precise, Fest's handiwork had left the victim's chest flat on the floor, but the startled, sneering face staring at the ceiling. Endelpo's head had been twisted completely backward. Both arms were clearly broken and folded at odd angles over his back. Johnny, it seemed, hadn't gotten as far as breaking the legs before Endelpo had either talked or died or both.

Omer swung his umbrella, paced, and thought. Then he hooked his umbrella on one arm and snapped on surgeon's gloves. He looked at the dates stamped on the lift tickets clipped to Endelpo's jacket and pulled an American Airlines ticket folder from the inside pocket. Then he checked the garage— empty, but still fragrant with exhaust. Well, it was obvious that Mr. Thuarte had just returned from a trip and that his luggage as well as his skis and car were nowhere about. This meant Johnny Fest was on his way, soon to switch cars probably, but on his way.

Omer went to Endelpo's study, which was littered with strewn files. Among shards of a broken lamp on the desk lay an address and appointment book, which was open to Sid Bifulco's new address. Taking out a small pad of his own, Omer took a few notes.

The next step was to call the police, anonymously identifying the killer and mentioning that he was probably driving a BMW with skis on the roof. It was a long shot.

After that, Omer was bound for Hellbender Eddy.

chapter 6

Saturday morning dawned over the Ballard Cabin porch, where Sid was splayed across a PVC chaise lounge like Robinson Crusoe tossed on the beach.

Soaked to the skin and damned near a broken man, he'd returned from his battle with the river and collapsed onto the plastic recliner. Sid's mind dived headfirst into exhausted sleep. Somewhere around two a.m. and in a fit of shivers, he had drawn the dusty spiral-weave rug from the porch floor over his sorry carcass.

Sid wasn't dreaming. He never had, not so he could remember. But as he stirred from soggy sleep in the predawn light, he felt positive the nuzzling in his ear was the tail end of some wicked slumber fantasy. There was a certain wuffling to the nuzzle, which he found disconcerting, and for some reason it made his nostril ache.

Rolling his head to the side, Sid found black squirrel pupils considering him with syncopated whisker spasms. Before the rodent could initiate a nasal probe, Sid slid his hand from beneath the rug and rotated it into a cup. The young squirrel found this of interest, climbed aboard Sid's hand, and began systematically inspecting each finger.

Sid's only warning was the flash of orange incisors.

Sharp pain and seconds later, Sid found himself sucking on a pinky, looking at a bunch of chattering leaves in the rafters. "Cute lil' mother," he mumbled around his pinky. "Painful, but cute."

In a matter of hours, Sid was refortified with new weapons, revised battle plans, sandwiches, coffee, some nylon rope, auxiliary oars, a new anchor, and a life preserver. He launched his boat again and rowed toward the bay below the rapids. His target: walleye at the near bank, on the outside of the bend, just like in the *Rod & Creel* illustrations.

The previous day's rain had brought the river up a few inches and left it cloudy. Starting from the tail of the rapids, Sid manned the anchor, drifting downriver and testing the depths. A knowing smile grew when the anchor suddenly found bottom much deeper. Just as he'd suspected—a nice drop-off where toothy walleye might prowl. The sun muscled by the loafing clouds and shone on the angler Bifulco. Anchor aweigh.

Walleye can be caught with jigs, doodads comprised of a hook with an oblong piece of painted lead at the head and a froufrou of feathers or hair at the tail. When bounced just off the bottom of a lake or river, the technique is aptly named jigging.

And so Angler Bifulco jigged. The current was constant, swirling but not fast, and he tossed his lures behind the boat and set the rods against the gunnels. The motion of the boat afforded a natural jigging action.

Puffs of cloud, like smoke from a cigar, filled the sky, and a breeze made the trees creak like the underside of a freight trestle. Before long, a brace of canoes drifted by, nice people waving and calling to him.

"Catch anything?" they all said.

"Sure," Sid replied over a mouthful of salami and rye. His rods pumped mildly in the rolling current, jigs dancing deep below.

Russ stood with a bucket on the rocky shoal near his landing and watched the intrepid Bifulco with a pair of binoculars.

"Well, I'll be damned. He's sitting on my walleye hole," Russ said aloud, lowering the binoculars. Too bad Sid hadn't been there earlier, trolling with Rapalas, Russ mused. Or later in the season, maybe using some lampers. If so, Sid might actually have had a chance. Probably turn up a shad though. Russ tucked the binoculars away and glanced upriver. It was nigh on ten a.m., and the weekend flotilla was on schedule.

There were a dozen or more canoe and rafting outfitters on the Upper Delaware, all of which launched several hundred craft encumbered with recreational boaters each spring and summer day. Now for some, a paddle down the scenic beauty of the Delaware has the emotional impact of a Frederic Church landscape. But for others, a paddle down the scenic Delaware is a notch up from beer slides at a frat wingding.

Russ could hear the hooting echo of the recreational boaters already. In honor of their arrival, he began turning over rocks along the shore looking for hellgrammites, black bi-pincered Dobson fly larvae as big as an index finger and doubtless the model for numerous alien sci-fi monsters. Great bait, but their ferocious pincers still made Russ a tad squeamish. He found courage in the fact that they were worth a quarter apiece.

When a flotsam of caterwauling oafs began to swirl around him, Sid merely sneered, noting, "There oughta be, like, some kind of a law against this shit."

But by eleven a.m., with the river a wall-to-wall yeasty commotion and discarded Bud Light cans, Sid was eager to commit an uncharacteristically messy homicide.

Canoes brimmed with sunburned, beefy Brooklynites. Inner tube swarms were plugged with guffawing jackanapes. Inflato-kayaks were draped with neon-bikinied jabbering flab. Floating coolers flocked about huge circular yellow rafts awash in bingeing servicemen on leave. Radios, boom boxes, banjos, and trumpets. Power squirters, Water Weenies, and Wonder Mud. Paddle splashing, capsizing, fisticuffs, and urinating.

After having his lines fouled, his bow slammed, and his neck popped by Water Weenie cross fire, Sid decided to weigh anchor and give it up. Just as he was leaning over the front of the boat, a buffoon suckling from a beer helmet zipped his runaway kayak down the fast current and fishtailed into the S.S. *Bifulco*.

Man overboard. The gang thought it was a scream.

A half hour later at Ballard Cabin, old boots, musty tarp, and oily rope flew out of the cedar closet as Sid searched in vain for a rifle. He had almost reached the point of lashing butter knives to broom handles before he simmered down and realized he might just jeopardize his parole if he speared a few recreational boaters.

chapter 7

At the New York Route 602 bridge over Char Brook, New York State Trooper Price was roused from deep contemplation by a speeding motorist. His radar gun flashed "70." A tan BMW with ski racks and Jersey plates was barreling west, Pennsylvania or bust.

Price groused as he put his cruiser in gear and sped after the violator. Every weekend, a vacationers' tide carried urbanites out to country homes, usually just up the road in Pennsylvania. It was on this New York approach to Frustrumburg that weekenders felt they were on the homestretch and could put the pedal to the metal. Thus the speed-trap vigil.

Trooper Price had a lot on his mind. A certain person whom he'd met at the bowling alley the night before called to tell him her bra was missing and reasoned it must still be in his car. That is, his wife's car, the one he drove to Friday Night League. The gnawing question had been whether he should return home and try to retrieve it, preferably without drawing attention to himself. But if Debbie had already found the bra, he had no ready excuse.

And it all depended on where the bra was. If it was wedged in the cushions, or under the seat, Debbie would not find it. She was eight months' pregnant and not likely to go snooping around the car's floor. On the other extreme, it was possible that the bra was in plain view. Price had been a little snookered, a little late, and in a little bit of a hurry when he got home. He might not have noticed it.

"Christ! It could be on the backseat," Price moaned for the umpteenth time that day, then flicked on his rollers.

His cruiser snapped up behind the BMW, which had slowed even before the red, white, and blue strobes came on. The motorist got brownie points for alertness and submissiveness.

But it took a blurp or two from the siren to get the BMW to pull over. Not uncommon. It was the "Who, *me*?!" routine, a ploy that made Price roll his eyes. But the vehicle did capitulate, making a right onto a narrow dirt clearing. The BMW pulled well away from the road, next to an abandoned fruit stand in a cornfield.

Collecting his citation book and ballpoint, Price

called in to report his doings. The dispatcher acknowledged, and mentioned that his wife had called and wanted him to phone home. 10–4.

Stepping out of the cruiser, the tall, square-shouldered trooper's mind was on only one thing: a big white brassiere. He removed his Smokey Bear hat and tossed it on the seat, his forearm mopping sweat from his brow, a hand running through his blond flattop. Price neglected to unclip his sidearm holster.

The driver's brawny arms were folded, and he looked up at Price from under a dark beetled brow.

At first Price was so distracted by the brassiere problem that he had to think what to say. Then it came to him.

"Did you know you were exceeding the speed limit, sir?" He noticed the guy was wearing a red and white striped shirt that was way too small for him, chest hair bulging out between the buttons.

A nickel-plated snubnose appeared in Johnny Fest's armpit.

There was a crack of gunfire and an echo. The BMW roared away leaving devils of dust in its wake and Price sprawled in the cornfield.

"What'll it be, mister?"

Omer was lost in admiring his surroundings, which reminded him of the old-time sandwich shops still found in the South. In point of fact, Omer thought it a dead ringer for the place where he'd met James Earl Ray in 1968. It was late morning, and the Five Star was empty. He targeted Chik with a congenial smile.

"Tea with lemon, please."

"Pie?" Chik clinked a teacup down at Omer's elbow.

"Sounds delicious, but no, thank you." Omer was readying to ask a question, but Chik headed him off.

"You, uh, just passing through or are you, uh, looking for anything—like antiques, directions... videos?" Chik squirted the countertop with seltzer from the fountain and began to mop it with his rag. He figured that any stranger was a possible referral for his sideline, video sales and rental. The naughty subject was awkward for strangers to broach. Then again, Chik thought this guy might be there because of those tapes he'd sent off to Venice, Florida. They were Chik's directorial debut, starring Chik and "Cherry," the persona Penelope from over at the Duck Pond had chosen. Chik always held out hope that he might be discovered as the porn artist he really was.

"Actually..." Omer flashed a gossiper's smile. "I am looking for someone." Omer bounced his eyebrows meaningfully. So did Chik, smoothing back his hair.

"Really? Maybe I can help you. Maybe, in fact, you've come to the right place." Chik winked, pouring hot tea into Omer's cup.

Omer leaned forward and looked both ways along the counter.

"Have you seen anyone new in town? A big fellow, probably a bit sweaty, with a city accent?"

Chik chewed on that a moment. He leaned on the rag and looked at the ceiling. Could this be some kinda double-talk? Sure—*Big & Sweaty*—that jived. It was one of the new titles in his last shipment—that is, the tape itself was "new in town." Boy, word sure got around fast sometimes. Chik snapped his fingers.

"*Big & Sweaty*. Sure, mister. That'll be seventeen fifty. Wait here, I'll go get it." Chik came around the counter and headed for the door. His Camaro was within spitting distance.

"Excuse me," Omer interjected. "Where are you going?"

"To the Camaro. It's in my trunk."

"Excuse me." Omer held up a finger. "You have him in your trunk?" Omer blinked.

"I have it in the trunk. *Big & Sweaty*, right?" Chik still had hold of the doorknob.

"Yes."

"It's in my trunk. What, don't you have the bucks?"

"Yes. But you keep saying 'it.' Last I knew, this man was a he."

"Lemme get this straight, mister. Do you want the videotape or what?"

"No, I'm looking for a man who's big and sweaty and just in town, probably at a motel."

Chik headed back behind the counter, waving one palm in the air.

"Hey, I don't know who sent you, buddy, but I only deal in food service and videos, man. I don't know who..."

"Could we start this all over again? I'm looking for a certain man who I think may have come this way. I'll gladly give you $17.50 if you'll tell me whether you've seen him. If not, I'd like you to keep an eye out for him. Should you actually identify him and verify that he was here, I'll give you a $50 bonus. The deal is all on the condition that you keep this quiet for twenty-four hours. If he's not here by then, he's not coming."

Chik played with the corner of a dishrag.

"How's that sound?" Omer persisted.

"Haven't seen him. Make it an even twenty up front, fifty later."

"Fine!" Omer smiled and put out a hand to shake on it.

When they'd parted paws, Omer whipped up one of his fatherly smiles and popped on his tweed crusher.

"I'll stop by later." He handed over a twenty. "Remember: big, sweaty, dark hair and eyes, city accent, dangerous."

"Got it." Chik immediately began to fold and crease the bill. "Hey, you sure you don't want any videos?"

Omer shook his head, winked, and peeled out the door.

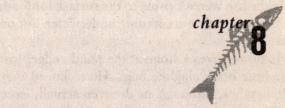

chapter **8**

Sid was at it again. He'd decided to take advantage of his very own trout pond. It was so small compared to the river, and calm, what could go wrong?

It was the middle of the afternoon. He stood on the breast of the elfin dam and gauged his target. His side of Ballard Pond was scrub and brush right up to the edge of the water. However, the opposite side was slightly higher and better groomed, presumably by that Smonig character. Sid assumed it was his neighbor's property, but just the same figured it was so high that a man standing there would spook the trout. *Sports Astream* had warned of such blunders, going so far as to suggest camouflage garb for an upstream approach in a thick fog.

Ballard Pond was smooth, dark, and quiet. The bottom of the pond, what he could see of it, was leaf laden but shallow enough to wade in hip boots a few feet from the edge. If he crouched and waded up his side of the pond, Sid guessed he'd be able to sneak up on them without the camouflage and also have some room to back cast.

As the fish weren't rising to the surface for food, Sid reasoned they were feeding underwater. But on what?

He turned over a stone at the pond's edge. Just some little black sluglike bugs. He reckoned they were nymphs, although he'd never actually seen any before, not in person. So he tied on a #14 Gold-Ribbed Black Nymph and moved from the dam and up along the leafy bank.

It was slow going. For one, the leaves and mud were deeper than he thought. For two, each mucky step spawned a great gray mushroom of mud. At least the current moved most of the murk behind him, toward the dam.

Ripples turned out to be the most difficult element to control. But without too much commotion, Sid got far enough up-pond so that he stood thigh deep and had room to cast without snagging bushes.

False casting, he got out thirty feet of line and let her rip. Nice cast. Nothing. His retrieve was impish little jerks, all the way to about five feet in front of him. Nothing. Another cast, another retrieve. Nothing.

"Psst."

Sid twisted around. It was Smonig, back by the willow. He was greasy up to the elbow and holding his truck's distributor. Sid scowled at him.

"Ducks..." Russ began in a stage whisper.

Sid held up an arresting hand and shook his head. No interruptions. Sid turned away.

Snubbed, Russ shrugged. He was just trying to tell Sid that a family of ducks had flown off the pond not fifteen minutes ago. The trout would be spooked from feeding for hours, though they might be tempted with worms or corn. Or maybe a little cheese. These trout were fresh from the stocking pond, and all they knew about food was what Purina put in a pellet. Russ ambled back toward the gaping gray jaws of his truck.

"Ducks. What I wanna hear about ducks? Can't he see I'm, like, busy?" Sid shook his head, but gave a glance back to see if Smonig was watching. Nope, the jerk was gone. Back to business.

Sid kept moving farther forward with the idea the fish were clustered closer to where the creek entered the pond. Trout always hang out in highly oxygenated water—*Rod & Creel* gospel—and usually that's where the water's splashing around, though sometimes it's where the water's real cold.

As Sid moved forward, he found himself creeping under the towering canopy of a pin oak. Unbeknownst to Sid, leaves dropped from the pin oak in great number each fall, and they accumulated directly beneath it in quantity. So much so, in fact, that they gave the false impression that the pond was shallower than it was.

In midcast, Sid brought a foot forward onto the oak leaf bottom, and his leg sank steadily into deep mud.

Anticipation swelled as the water topped his hip boot and loaded his leg with thirty pounds of cold brown scum, bubbles of methane filling his nostrils with a horsy stench. The leg kept going down, and the chilly water approached his groin. Reflexively, he raised his arms over his head and started sucking in air, as though that might somehow make him lighter.

Like a bug on flypaper or a mouse on a glue trap, Sid brought the other foot forward to pull the sinking one out.

Chest deep in mud and chin deep in water, it was beginning to dawn on him that there were a lot more angles to this angling business than he'd figured.

There was only one way out. He had to bid farewell to the hip boots, unclip them, slither free, and make like a mudskipper by wallowing to the shore generously slathered in fetid mud. Once free of them, however, Sid couldn't resist trying to recover his hip boots.

Plastered hat to socks in muck, Sid stomped toward Ballard Cabin, rod in one hand and a lone hip boot in the other. A twist to the spigot knob

brought a hose to life, and he rinsed off both himself and his gear. Then he headed for the shower inside.

That's where Sid learned about the little black
"nymphs." Bugs they were not. Leeches they were.

chapter
9

For those who think four-dollar pitchers are only
served in heaven at a tavern with a ten-cent jukebox, the Duck Pond is cloud nine. Yuengling is
served in smooth-sided fifty-two-ounce pitchers,
and a 1964 jukebox plays a single for a dime.
Album sides are four bits.

What with the advent of compact discs, though,
the music at the Duck Pond was limited largely
to pre-1990 tunes. Nobody seemed to notice. Certainly not Big Bob. His favorite band was Boston,
the Doobies taking a close second. And as it happened, Big Bob was personally responsible for wearing the Boston *Boston* album smooth, at a cost
variously estimated by regulars to be somewhere
between two and three hundred dollars' worth of
plays. The demise of that first album came as a relief

to some, but soon thereafter Big Bob supplied his own copy of Boston's second album, *Don't Look Back*. Having drawn the short drink stirrer, Russ was picked by fate to tell Big Bob that he was limited to one play and one side of *DLB* a night.

Everybody was sure Big Bob would be emotionally crushed. And in turn, they were sure Russ would be physically crushed. Contrary to popular speculation, though, Bob took it very well. In fact, he was quite moved that Russ was such an up-front kinda guy. And as it happened, Big Bob came to consider Russ his barroom sage on matters of the heart, though matters of intellect were still the realm of *Newstime* magazine.

"So she looks at me kinda funny. I don't know how to describe it, Russ. She wuzn't laughin' at me, but she wuzn't takin' it real serious. Do ya think maybe she thinks I'm too big for her?" Big Bob sloshed some more Yuengling in Russ's mug, then his own. They sat at a pedestal table with a flecked plastic top. A wagon wheel chandelier bedecked in illuminated plastic duck decoys hung overhead.

"What can I tell you, Bob? Louise is four foot ten and you're six foot five. What would you do if a girl eight feet tall asked you out?" Russ was already looking around for a way out of the heart-to-heart. He really wanted to huddle with motor-head Lloyd over the International's distributor troubles.

"That's different. Guys is supposed to be taller'n the gal anyways. Besides, we're talking about people at normal sizes." Bob stared at his beer and tried to

decide when he wanted his *DLB* album side—
sooner or later.

"O.K., Bob, point taken, but I was after your gut
reaction. Someone who's big is a little intimidat-
ing, that's all. Hey, whatever happened to that girl
Maria, the timberman on that bridge job of yours?
She's five eleven." A ray of hope—Lloyd had just
strolled in with Kris. If Russ could only catch his
eye, get him to come over and sit down, Bob would
probably withdraw to the jukebox.

"Nothin' happened to Maria. The point is, Russ,
I like the little ones, whut can I tell ya, and I don't
think it's fair that just because I'm the size I am, I
can't find a small girl. Why, I remember reading in
Newstime, October of '85, a feature on midgets and
dwarfs and stuff—how that little guy from *Fantasy
Island*—he married a girl who was twice his size.
And so did a lot of those fellahs. All real normal
relationships too. Now why can't it happen th'other
way around? Russ?"

A dark look shadowed Bob's brow. Russ jumped
back on track.

"Yes, but what you've got to realize, Bob, is that
if you're going to create a narrow set of parameters,
no matter what they are—say, you insisted on a girl
with an I.Q. of 180—there are going to be fewer
who meet the requirements. You're going to have to
maybe ask out twice the number of small girls before you find one who's not intimidated by your rel-
ative sizes and before you come up with a winner.

Hullo, Lloyd!" Russ shrugged at Bob, who was still entrenched in his dilemma.

"How ya guys doing?" Lloyd gave a knowing look to Russ. "Hey, Big Bob, how's the pile-driving? Could you do me a favor? Can you get Little Bob to stop callin' me Doc? It really bugs me the way he keeps callin' me Doc. Say, ya look in a glum mood there tonight, Big Bob."

"It's nothing, Lloyd, probably just thinkin' too much. I'll talk with Cropsey about callin' ya Doc. He's got a kinda inconsiderate side, that's all." Bob stepped out of and over his chair, headed for the jukebox. "If you guys'll excuse me, I'm gonna go look at the tunes."

"Thanks, Lloyd." Russ sloshed some Yuengling into his savior's glass.

Lloyd tilted his head in Big Bob's direction. "Girl trouble again?"

"Girl trouble always. It's not that I don't care, but it's always the same thing." Russ rolled his eyes.

"Uh-huh. Like a guy I know. All he ever wants to talk about is the trouble with his confounded International Harvester pickup." Lloyd grinned, stroking his Vandyke.

"Hey, I don't always . . ."

"You're right. Last time it was the Dodge. I still say that if you clean your battery posts the Dodge would start right up."

"Doubtful, Lloyd. Battery posts aside, it hasn't been run in five months."

"So what's with the International?"

"Distributor."

Lloyd's gal Kris stepped up, a sharp, petite woman with short-short dusty brown hair. Big Bob always tried not to look at her.

"Ya fellahs motor-headin'? Ugh. Look, I'm gonna beat Penelope in Duck Hunt. Spare some quarters, handsome? Russ, honey? Ya eatin' all right? Ya look tired."

"I'm up at four-thirty about five days a week. When am I not tired, Kris?" Russ smiled.

Kris just shook her worried face at Russ and took the two crumpled greenbacks Lloyd was surrendering.

"A man your age." With that, Kris trotted over to the Duck Hunt machine where the chocolate brunette Penelope snapped Bazooka and swayed to the Doobies, which had just come on the jukebox. The strains of "Jesus Is Just Alright with Me" swirled a bit of soul in the bar. Penelope had just gotten off work. The management at The Pond only needed a waitress for the lunch crowd. There was no dinner crowd.

"Kris has a mind to fix the sad state of your love life, Russ." Lloyd clicked a plastic-tipped cheroot in his teeth.

Russ put one hand over his heart, the other in the air while admiring Penelope's behind. She was shooting video ducks, a light pistol on one hip and a hand in the back pocket on the other. "Still trying to fix me up? I'm a duly deputized bachelor, Lloyd. Can't she accept that?"

"In a word? Nope. And I think she's still working on you an' Penelope." Lloyd flicked a lighter in the vicinity of his cheroot while also admiring Penelope's behind, her pelvis twitching with each pistol blast. "And of course I'm still trying to work on what I gotta do to get that musky."

"I told you, a tune-up on my..."

"A tune-up isn't what ya need, Russ, I keep tellin' ya that. Ya need to stop messin' with your fuel mixture."

"But I read somewhere that if you put a little less oil in the gas and adjust the mixture screw..."

"Look, Russ, let me get rid of some of that ear hair."

"Ear hair?" Russ grabbed at his ears.

"Yeah, it's comin' in. Ya got one big black curly one right..."

"Ho, Smonig," Sid interrupted. He jerked up a chair from the next table and sat. "Mind if I sit down?"

"Oh, er, hullo!" Russ lowered his hands from his ears. "Uh, Lloyd, I'd like you to meet my new neighbor, Sid Bifulco."

Sid considered Lloyd's outstretched hand a moment, shook it with obvious disinterest, and focused back on Russ. "Yeah, nice t'meet you. Can I buy you guys a Canadian?"

"Careful, Sid," Lloyd piped up. "Offers like that are always accepted around here."

Sid barely glanced in Lloyd's direction as he pointed a ten-dollar bill at him. "Then I guess you won't mind bein' a good boy an' gettin' us the round." Sid smiled at Russ.

Lloyd shrugged and headed for the bar. A guy who bought the drinks got special license to be drunk, stupid, or obnoxious.

"So, how was Ballard Pond?" Russ sat across from Sid. "Get any?"

Sid's expression was fixed, but a bloody tint rose across what looked like two tiny hickeys on his neck, over his angular jaw, and up to his silver-tinged hairline.

"To be perfectly honest, Smonig, not so friggin' good."

"Uh-huh. Well, I didn't mean to bother you out there, but I was trying to—"

"Smonig, that Trout Lady tells me you're some kinda fishing expert around here. That right?"

"Well, I do a little guiding, tie a lotta flies, write . . ."

"Don't let him fool ya, Sid." Lloyd returned with the drinks. They poured them fast and sloppy at The Pond. "Russ here's the local guru. Everybody around the Eddy tries to pump him for info on the hot spots. But Russ here's got a price. Why, ya should have heard the little speech he made at the Five Star."

"You got a price, Smonig?" With the smooth sweep of a magician, Sid used one hand to pluck his own drink and hold out the other for Russ.

"I charge by the half day, seventy-five dollars."

"Seventy-five bucks, huh, for a half day?" Sid

tugged pensively at an earlobe. "Tell me, Smonig, how many kinds of fish can you go for in half a day?"

Russ sipped his drink and winced from the bite. Though he liked it well enough, whisky was the exception rather than the rule. It wasn't in his budget.

"Hm. Maybe two or three, but generally a client is after something in particular, like trout."

"And how many kinds of fish, fished for in all the different ways you can fish for 'em, are there around here?"

Confused, Russ blinked, then went to put his drink on the table but didn't. "Huh? I don't follow."

"Don't ya get it, Russ?" Lloyd interjected, snapping his cheroot at the ashtray. "Our new neighbor here is trying to figure out how many half days it would take to learn everything ya know about fishing around here."

Casting an eye in Lloyd's direction, Sid smirked, reached out a hand, and gripped Lloyd's shoulder.

"You're a sharp guy, Louie." Sid gave Lloyd's shoulder a few hard squeezes and let go. Lloyd puffed at his cheroot somewhat uneasily. "You got another of them there wheezers, Louie?"

"Wheezer?"

"Yeah, a cigar?"

"Oh, uh, sure." Lloyd handed one over.

"And a light?" Sid tilted his head back and to the side.

"Oh, yeah, sorry." Lloyd lit Sid's cigar.

Sid drew deeply and with obvious satisfaction on the cheap cigar. "Russ, I like your friend Louie."

"Yup, Louie is kinda handy to have around, I guess," Russ mumbled uneasily.

"Louie's kinda, I dunno—whatsit the French say? A certain *I dunno what*? Anyhow, when you figure out your price, Smonig, swing by for a drink." Scooting his chair out, Sid got to his feet and downed his Canadian. He set his glass on a folded ten. "Have another round on me, boys. Adios." He ran his fingers through his hair, instinctively checking his peripheral vision as he walked from the dark barroom into twilight.

No sooner had Sid stiff-armed the front door than Big Bob stomped over to the slack-jawed Russ and Lloyd.

"Hey, Russ, who was that guy?" Bob helped himself to the pitcher.

"My new neighbor," Russ said absently. "Moved into the Ballard place."

"Guy sure looks familiar. Like an actor or something."

Little Bob, his wife, Val, and his camcorder had just arrived. The latter was zooming in on Russ, Lloyd, and Big Bob.

"Or 'something' is about like it!" Lloyd started to chortle through his cigar smoke.

Russ gave a short laugh and mugged Sid's half-lidded, smooth demeanor.

"Yo, Louie, you got another of them wheezers?"

"Sure, boss!" Lloyd unwrapped a cheroot and fit it in Russ's mouth.

"Hey, guys, this is great! Doc, turn toward the camera." Little Bob danced around for a better vantage.

"Bob, must you?" Val tugged at Little Bob's shirtsleeve.

"Don't call me Doc!" Lloyd moaned.

"I guess I'll have to get my own spritzer," Val chirped, drifting over to the bar.

"Light me, Louie!" Russ commanded through clenched teeth.

"Yes, Mr. Sid! Right away, Mr. Sid!" Lloyd chirped.

Russ blew out a cloud of smoke, reached back, and grabbed Lloyd by the beard. He gave it a waggle.

"Louie, you're a peach!"

They disintegrated in laughter, which drew Kris and Penelope over to the table, whereupon the scene was replayed. Lively discussion accompanied ever more beer on their pal Sid's ten. Before too long, Kris and Penelope played out their version of the scene, then Big and Little Bob were goaded into a stilted production that brought the house down. Every five minutes someone would inevitably blurt: "Light me, Louie!" and grab Lloyd by the beard. Big Bob got a share of the kidding over his contention that Sid was someone he'd seen before, a famous person.

Somewhere along the line Val traded Little Bob a

dirty look for the car keys and snuck out. She was never much for barroom antics, especially what with the next day being Church Day.

The party marched on for a few hours, and Russ's hoarse giggles were worn to tatters by the time the gang stumbled from the Duck Pond at last call. However, his taste for speculation on Sid was not exhausted. As they split for their respective pickup trucks and SUVs, the battle cry went up: "Light me, Louie! You're a peach!" Rambunctious plumes of cold fog billowed from the revelers' lips into the harsh beams of the parking lot flood lamps. The spring night had taken on a chill, and the moon had not yet risen.

Russ chuckled gently and fumbled with his keys in the shadow of his truck.

A heavy hand landed on his shoulder.

"Russ, ya O.K. to drive? Ya know, statistics show that most accidents at night are alcohol-related."

"Look, Bob, are you any soberer than me?" Russ eyed his giant friend.

"I think so. I didn't have any of that Canadian. Too many free radicals in blended whiskys," Bob warned.

"Uh-huh. Well, if you drive me, how are you gonna drive your Bronco?" Russ held up a key and opened the driver's door.

"Little Bob—he never drinks anything much—he an' me is together since Val took his sedan." Bob held the car door open without effort as Russ climbed in and tried to pull the door closed.

"O.K., look, I appreciate the concern." Russ tugged at the door and almost pulled himself from the truck to the parking lot. Bob still held it open. "O.K., look, I'll drive, O.K., an' you ride with me an' make sure I drive O.K. all the way home. See, this truck, well, y'know it's got kinda funny steering and stuff."

Little Bob pulled up in Big Bob's Bronco, camcorder on the seat beside him.

Big Bob nodded. "O.K., Russ. But ya so much as swerve and we stop. I ain't lettin' ya kill me."

On the way down 241, Russ kept a steady hand, and Big Bob only felt obliged to comment on maintaining the speed limit.

"Y'know, Russ, in almost eighty percent of all accidents after dark, excessive speed is listed as a secondary cause of accident."

Russ nodded in the milky glow of the dashboard. "I did not know that, Bob. Say, Bob, who do you think this guy Bifulco is? A TV personality? What?" A glance in the rearview confirmed Little Bob was right behind.

"Dunno, but I don't never forget faces. I coulda used a good look at him. The ducks don't put out much light. It's not exactly well lit at the bar."

"Do you think if you got a better look it might come back to you?"

"Might. Might."

"Well, let's say we go take a look."

"Tonight?"

*   *   *

As the International veered up Ballard Road from 241, Russ gave the tan BMW parked on the shoulder only passing notice.

"Shhh. We're gonna sneak up on Ol' Sid, see if you recognize him. Don't want the headlights to flash his cabin as I come down my drive." Russ killed the headlights.

"Russ..."

"Bob, I know every inch of this drive." He glanced in the rearview mirror. Little Bob had gone to his parking lights.

"You're goin' a little fast there, partner," Big Bob warned.

Russ tugged the wheel left, neatly turning the International down the shadowy slope of his driveway.

Impact. Quaking metal racked the front of the truck; a crack split across the windshield. Standing on the brake, Russ locked the wheels and the International skewed, grinding to a stop on the side of the drive. The Bronco's orange parking lights swerved around them to the left.

Steam jetted from the truck's groaning radiator.

Russ was still gripping the wheel, and Bob had his outstretched hands on the dashboard.

Tinkling shards of glass falling from a headlamp flooded the sudden silence.

Russ and Bob looked at each other.

"I'd say ya hit somethin'," Bob said.

Russ could see his International's hood was

creased dead center, like cake icing smooshed by an ogre's finger.

In front of them, Little Bob put the Bronco in drive, pulled on the headlights, and began a three-point turn in front of Russ's trailer.

"It was a deer, I think. We ran it over." Russ reached for the door handle, but hesitated. "I felt it go down."

"A bear, ya think?" Big Bob grabbed his door handle, paused, then wrenched it open. "Messed up your radiator, that's for sure."

Russ emerged slowly, just as the Bronco's headlights came to bear on him and the obscuring cloud of Prestone fog that geysered from his grille. Plumes swirled over the truck.

Little Bob climbed out of the Bronco and joined Big Bob and Russ. The three stood staring at the wisps and tumbles of steam that rolled through the headlights' glare.

Big Bob held a shading hand to his brow and scanned the ground around Russ's truck. "I don't see nothin'."

Russ didn't see anything either. But he was too scared to say anything.

Little Bob put his camcorder on the ground, got on all fours, and looked under the truck.

"Oh boy, oh boy..."

Russ and Big Bob got on all fours. The view under the truck was obscured by steam. At first. Then the clouds parted. They could see arms. And a red and white striped shirt.

"Holy bejesus, Russ!" Big Bob smacked himself in the head.

"Man, oh man!" Little Bob put a hand over his eyes.

Russ suddenly found himself in a pastry shop, sticking his finger into slices of strawberry pie while the girl at the register—Penelope?—was distracted by a pink parrot, squawking "Light me, Louie!"

Russ's fainting spell lasted a minute or so. Long enough for help to arrive. Someone was pinching his nose. Pastries, parrots, and Penelope vaporized, and his neighbor Sid, wearing a red satin bathrobe, was leaning over him.

"Congratulations, Smonig." Sid grinned. "You, my friend, are a murderer."

chapter

10

"My way is the only way, believe me, Smonig. I know how to get away with murder." Sid put a mug of instant coffee in front of Russ, who hadn't made a peep since leaving the confectionary and entering Sid's cabin.

But Sid had been doing plenty of peeping, enough for both of them, and for the Bobs too. Sid wasn't sure he was getting through to Russ, so he set it out for him again.

"You got a blood alcohol level that'd get you busted for sure. Nothin' you can do about that for maybe six hours. By that time, if you call the cops then, delayed like, they'll figure something don't smell good. And when they find out you was in a bar all night, forget about it. And who was this schmoe anyways? Do you know him? Well, as it so happens, I do know him. He's a no-good louse—a crook and a rapist."

"Hey!" Big Bob snapped from a daze and struggled out of the musty plaid couch. "Russ, ya know who Sid is? He's Sid Bifulco!"

Russ just stared at the tabletop. Sid sucked his teeth and folded his arms.

"Sure, he's Sid Bifulco! Ya know, that guy!" Big Bob spun around and looked at the other drowsy Bob.

"Don't ya get it, he's, like, a mobster. They called him 'Sleep' 'cause he put a guy out before killing him. Ya killed like, what was it?" Big Bob snapped his fingers at "Sleep."

Sid brushed at a lapel.

"Convicted of ten murders." Sid held up ten digits for all to see.

"Ten guys! He killed ten guys! But he got outta prison 'cause he ratted—oh, sorry..." Big Bob bowed to his host apologetically.

Little Bob came alive, jumping to his feet. "Yes, yes, that's it—you're right! I remember." But when Sid glanced at him, Little Bob sat right back down like he'd spoken out of turn.

It didn't bug Sid that they knew his past. In fact, being a murderer engendered a special kind of respect, an esteem that he sorely missed. Sid reclaimed the stage.

"There you have it, Russ." Sid snapped his fingers in the Bobs' direction. "A watchamacallit, a testimonial. As my lawyer Endelpo would say, 'I have many years' experience in these matters.' Russ, listen t'me—that crumb you just crushed?—yeah, his name is Jimmy...eh...Spaghetti. He was the kinda lowlife you couldn't avoid in my line of work."

"Spaghetti?" Little Bob jumped up. "His name was Spaghetti, like with meatballs?"

Sid winced, trying to stay focused on his yarn. "So this Spaghetti guy was bad. A burglar, and a rapist when opportunity knocked. He liked coming out here to lonely cabins with old ladies in 'em. Jimmy had what you'd call a special fondness for old ladies. Not a pretty character, believe you me. BUT!" Sid pressed his hands together prayer-style, pointing them at Russ.

"BUT...here you come with your truck and a snootful. Good thing or bad thing?"

"Bad thing!" Little Bob threw up his hand from the sofa, but the teacher ignored him.

"You actually done a *good* thing, Russ." Sid chuckled, parting his hands as if revealing the truth. "Not only did you whack a real scumbag, but you saved the taxpayers an awful lotta money by puttin' him in the flower bed. The trial an' all, what would that cost? Unbelievable! We're talking hundreds of thousands of dollars! Maybe millions. And all that green for a guy like that?"

"He's right, Russ." Big Bob stepped up next to Sid. "Ya know it costs somethin' like twenty-five grand a year to keep a guy in prison? And your average felony conviction costs somethin' like a half million dollars or more. That comes outta our taxes."

"See, Russ, the big guy knows." Sid patted Big Bob on the arm then crouched in front of Russ trying to catch his gaze.

"Now look at me, for instance. I murdered ten guys—maybe a lot more, ones they never knew about. An' I'm outta the joint. How long do you think this guy Jimmy...eh...Spaghetti would stay in the pen, if convicted?"

"The average prison time served for a rapist is only like two years, Russ," Big Bob agreed. "For burglary maybe less than a year on a first conviction."

Sid jerked a thumb at Big Bob.

"Big Guy's right. I'm right. Hey, you..."

Little Bob, still cuddling his camcorder, rose and took small steps toward Sid like he was approaching the principal's desk.

"Yeah, I'm talkin' to you. Whadda you think? Was getting run over by Russ too good for that no-good-bag-of-shit Jimmy or what?" Sid waved a hand in Little Bob's direction.

"Did you really kill ten people?"

Sid turned his head and smiled directly at Little Bob. "Whadda you think?"

"Wow. If, if as he says, Russ, the guy wuz like a rapist...Old ladies, Russ!" Little Bob winced, and took his seat.

Sid focused back on Russ.

"You see, Russ? It's not a bad thing you done.

Now I ask you: will the police see it that way? No, they won't see it that way. All they know is you were DWI. And the shame of it all is you'd throw your life away on a scumbag like Spaghetti."

"Please shut up!" Russ slammed his coffee mug on the table. To Russ, a disaster like running down and killing Jimmy Spaghetti was the last straw. This was the final smashup in a life of roadway disasters. He had tried to break the cycle, tried to extinguish the fire of Sandra's death, tried to flee doubting friends and family in Hartford. Russ had made a clean break by embracing the supposedly simple rural life. Somewhere along the line, though, somewhere during those ten years since Sandra's death, the specter of the fiery ravine was supposed to have dissolved.

It had been hand to mouth all the way. Russ was always one catastrophe away from ruin. He needed to win big for a change, to break free. But now freedom from his curse seemed utterly hopeless.

Russ's doom shadowed the room like an eclipse. Sid got up and walked out. In a minute, he came back dressed in slacks, windbreaker, and sport shirt. Over one arm was a drop cloth, some clothesline, and a coil of oily hemp rope he'd scavenged from the cedar closet. In one hand was a glass of water, and in the other hand were two white tablets. He pulled up next to Russ.

"Here."

Russ took the pills, took the water. He hoped "Sleep" had struck again.

"You guys watch him 'til he drops off. Then you can beat it. He'll sleep on my couch for the night." Sid went out the front door.

First and foremost, the package was wrapped burrito-style in a tarp, preferably waterproof. Next, the package was bound tightly with rope to insure that there was no unraveling. These preliminaries served the purpose of containing incriminating fluids and fibers, loose personal effects, ungainly snagging limbs, and stray rotting tidbits down the line. It also facilitated handling, dragging, and dropping.

But without assistance, getting the package into the trunk was problematic. Johnny Fest was a good 6'4" and 280 pounds. Sid could lift the feet, but not the torso.

Sid was not without a few tricks of his trade. He dragged his package beneath a nearby tree and tossed a rope over a limb. One end was tied off at Big Bob's front bumper, the other at Fest's chest. The bumper groaned, the limb creaked, the rope stretched and frayed. Sid backed up Big Bob's Bronco about eight feet and stopped. What with the stretch in the rope and the bending tree limb, Fest's belly dangled only three feet off the ground. His toes touched dirt. But it was enough so that when Sid backed his white Ford LTD up to him he could push on the soles of Johnny's tarped feet and fold the package headfirst into the trunk.

Just like old times. With Johnny in the trunk, Sid drove to a construction site he'd noticed where Route 241 passed over a swampy gorge about ten miles north of Frustrumburg.

Pillars for the new Route 241 bridge had concrete foundations that extended some distance into the ground. These foundations were made by driving tapered steel cylinders into the earth and filling them with concrete. Pile drivers were used to pound these steel cylinders into the ground, and they were noticeable to Sid because of the height of their substantial derricks. And because they signaled a great place to dump a body.

Jagged cerise of sunrise tinged the horizon where the low clouds had started to break. Out of the night, icy raindrops beat a slow tap, then a drumroll on the plywood that covered the steel pile casing. Sid shoved the plywood to one side and looked down the casing. Bottomless to the eye. He left one end of the rope secured around his package, then tossed the other end over a steel pole above the casing, then tied that end to his bumper. He drove twenty feet forward, the rope pulled the package from the trunk, and he heard a dull thump. Stepping out of the LTD into a steady rain, Sid unfolded a pocketknife and looked down at Fest dangling in the gloom of the casing. He drew the blade across the rope, it snapped, the package dropped feetfirst. There was a sound not too unlike the snapping of ice trays when it hit bottom.

"Couldn't happen to a nicer guy," Sid smirked,

drawing a sleeve over his wet face. Several buckets full of gravel dumped in atop the package assured that nobody would notice it eighty-five feet down. Sid retrieved his rope, replaced the plywood cover, and drove home. All that was left was to deep-six Fest's stolen BMW in the woods somewhere, and then Sid could catch some winks.

chapter **11**

The second week of May arrived the next morning with all horns blaring. A warm high-pressure front had rolled the cold air back to the north, stretching the sky in great flourishing streaks of stratospheric mares' tails. Cool maroon shadows carpeted Hellbender Eddy; a hot purplish sky contrasted neon overhead.

Though Russ awoke from a dreamless night to the smell of fried ham, coffee, and cinnamon rolls, and even though he actually felt well rested, he remembered what had happened the night before. He lay there on Sid's couch, a blanket pulled up to his nose, staring at the ceiling: police should have been called, eternal irrevocable shame and doom averted. He could hear Sid knocking around the kitchen, whistling tunelessly as a Frank Sinatra CD played.

The percolator slurped along, but out of sync with "One for My Baby."

As if he'd heard Russ's eyes open, Sid marched into the living room, yanked on the curtain drawstring, and cranked open the picture window.

"C'mon, get up. C'mon, c'mon—outside, c'mon..."

Sid poked and jostled Russ out the front door, spooking a tizzy of skippers from the daffodils next to the cabin. They marched off the portico and into the side yard, where Sid planted Russ and squared his shoulders. Russ stood squinting uneasily at the river, wiggling his toes in tube socks wet from the grass.

Many people would have liked to believe that men like Sid Bifulco were criminally insane, that they were, in point of fact, evil. Could sane, rational, emotionally balanced people murder? And yet there were model citizens who made a living crawling through sewers, eviscerating cattle, or performing autopsies on putrefied remains. Perhaps people could sanely do almost anything, irrespective of good or bad, revolting or repugnant, violent or vile, if it was suitably rationalized. For some, killing was not evil, rather the apotheosis of rationality, in that death is inevitable, final, and ultimately irrelevant.

This was not to say murder came easily to an otherwise sane person. For Sid, it was difficult the first few times. But as death became familiar, it almost rationalized itself, a process often facilitated with some spiritual guidance. And in the insular world of wiseguys, there was often an old hand to point out the path to vindication.

"Russ, look at the tree, the big, sticky, Christmas-type tree over my cabin. It's alive, am I right? Now the cabin. What's it made of, Russ? It's made of logs, am I right? Now think about this: do the logs know they're dead?"

Russ just blinked. It was occurring to him that whenever Sid opened his mouth, Russ felt like he'd just smoked a joint.

"Now think about this. Did you ever notice the logs was dead? No, you didn't, did you? O.K., now look at the river. Look at it. What is it? I'll tell you what it is. It's a bunch of water rolling down the hill toward Trenton. Think about this, Russ. How long has this river been flowing? Long before Trenton was ever there, am I right? Long before you an' me was born. Maybe before anybody was born, anybody at all. And I'll tell you something, Russ. It'll be flowing a long time after everybody dies. A long time after this cabin rots away. A long time after this big Christmas tree is nothing but mulch. And nobody—nobody, Russ—will even remember they was here. But they was alive once, and that's the only thing that ever matters to the tree, and the logs back when they was alive. So let's go have breakfast."

Russ stood in the side yard for some minutes after Sid had gone inside, a bit dazed and decidedly confused. Whatever Sid was on about, it sounded like it should make sense. Eventually Russ turned, went in, sat down at a card table on the screened porch, and ate breakfast in silence.

He cut through two slabs of ham and three cinnamon rolls, and as he raced Sid on a third cup of coffee, the sun crested the opposite bank of the river, filling the porch from the top down with lemony spring light.

Russ cleared his throat. "Where is he, Sid?"

Sid was eating a cinnamon roll with a knife and fork. He didn't even miss a beat.

"He's gone, Russ, plain and simple. I took him away where he'll rest for all time. I took him to where only God can find him, and you can be damned sure he will too. Where he goes after God gets through with him?" Sid pointed his fork at the floor and winked at Russ.

"Anyways, I figure we'd do a little fishing today. My idea—well, what I'd like to start with is smallmouth bass." Sid lifted the percolator to fill their mugs. His parole officer, the guy who expected "bronze backs," was sure to be his first visitor, and he knew it'd be important to impress upon him how well he was fitting back into society.

"But what about—"

"Your friends? Your friends are good people, Russ. They understand. Last night you hit a tree. See?"

Russ pivoted, and through a hole in the bushes next to the pin oak on Ballard Pond he could see his truck, the front wrapped around a tree.

"A tree?"

"Sure." Sid wiped his mouth with a napkin, sniffed, and scooted out his chair. "C'mon."

A leisurely stroll across the Ballard dam breast to Russ's yard and driveway took them to where the truck was firmly pressed into a tree. The bark was torn and everything.

Leading him to the passenger side, Sid wrenched the door open with difficulty and ushered Russ into the driver's seat.

"A tree," Russ mumbled, almost believing—almost. After all, he hadn't seen the actual collision. It could have been a tree, couldn't it? The sun was as bright and blinding as the night had been dark and ominous.

"You hit a tree, Russ. I think a mechanic'll find that your steering box cracked when you turned the wheel and the gears locked, seized up, and was steered right into the tree. You're a lucky guy. You mighta been hurt. Big Bob said he'll send a truck over to tow this beast into the shop for repairs—on me. I can't stand to watch you mess with that truck on such a beautiful day. Besides, you an' me got a deal. I helped you with your problem. You help me with mine. Now let's go fishing, huh, Russ?"

Omer had his Karmann Ghia pointed back to New York when he stopped at a pay phone next to a general store whose side advertised "Mail Pouch Chewing Tobacco." He hadn't seen one of those since he hooked up with Arthur Bremer at a covered bridge outside Milwaukee in 1972. And to think with four bullets Bremer couldn't kill Democratic candidate George Wallace. Well, four more shell casings for Omer's collection.

"Hullo." The background clatter was either that of a bottling plant or a bowling alley.

"It's Mr. Phillips. Good news. Johnny Fest is out of the game, permanently. Believe it or not, he had an accident—run over by a truck." Omer pushed back his wool crusher and let the sun warm his face.

"As long as it's fixed, that's all. Who did the job?"

"A neighbor—name of Russ Smonig—ran him over with a truck when he came home last night. Fest was just approaching our Bifulco's cabin, and I was in position to intervene..." Omer filled his nostrils with the heady fumes of warm morning grass.

"What was the name again? Spell it."

"Who? The neighbor in the truck?"

"Spell it."

"R-U-S-S S-M-O-N-I-G."

"I'll call from another number, in a little bit. Don't move." The line went dead.

Omer dangled the receiver by a single index finger before sending it home. The store was closed Sundays, but some loose change got him a Hires from a bottled pop machine. Been ages since he'd seen one of those. It reminded him of a cold Sunday in Harlem, a gas station, and a meeting with Talmadge Hayer. Now there was a fellow who knew how to do the job. He not only blasted Malcolm X with a shotgun, but then others stepped up with pistols and finished him off. The shells from that incident took up almost a whole shelf.

Sitting on the edge of his blue sports car, he drank his Hires and didn't think about what had made his employer nervous. Omer had learned long ago not to ask too many questions, even if only of himself.

A crow plunked down on a crab apple tree across the road and surveyed the stranger with a jocular eye. Arching an eyebrow at his audience, Omer watched as the crow hopped to another branch, cocked its head at him, and stood on one leg. The bird's beak was open, and its red dagger tongue flicked as though it was about to say something.

The pay phone rang, breaking the staring match. Omer climbed the porch.

"We got problems, Mr. Phillips." A steady hiss and racket punctuated the statement. Sounded like a body shop.

"Problems are my business." The crow started to make excited, dice-in-a-cup sounds behind Omer's back.

"There's a contract out on this Smonig guy. Has been for ten years."

Omer pulled the receiver away and looked at the handset like it had licked him. A contract on Smonig? "What do you want me to do?"

"For now, just listen. You remember anything about Georgi Ristocelli and a pal gettin' gunned down in front of Neglio's in Hartford? Five guys pulled the job. You and I are interested in the welfare of one of 'em, though he didn't touch a trigger. Well, do you also remember how there was all kindsa witnesses that the cops have been looking for ever since?"

"Yes, I remember. It's been on television, I think."

"You bet it was, on that show *Mug Shots*. They reenacted the whole thing just recently, said how they was looking for those same witnesses. But just between you, me, an' the wall, we happen to know they'll never find those witnesses."

"I see," Omer said flatly. He didn't want to seem too interested. Frankly, he wasn't.

"No, you don't see, Mr. Phillips. One of these witnesses was a young woman named Sandra Jones, who as it happens was this guy Smonig's wife."

"I see."

"Sure, they made it look like an accident, like the steering went out on her car, but this guy Russell was thrown clear of the wreck and survived. Said he saw someone at the wreck with a gun who called him Evel Knievel. It was Smonig's contention that somebody had messed with the steering box. Nobody bought it. Her family, his family was all burned up at him for makin' the fuss, an' suddenlike he's gone. Which suited us fine. The contract was pretty much a 'when or where'—no big deal, so it's kinda forgot, what with inflation and all. And now, since the Palfutti family is history...

"The deal is this: we don't think she ever told him about bein' a witness or he woulda used that t'convince the cops she was whacked. Yeah. He couldn't see too good after the wreck, but he might recognize our friend as the guy who showed up with the gun. If not now, maybe later. An' he might start askin' questions. I dunno. Anyhow, I guess our friend don't recognize Smonig either."

"I see." Omer did, finally, see.

"A delicate matter, Mr. Phillips. We don't want anything to upset our friend's retirement, make him seek out the Witness Protection Program, maybe cut some more deals with the Feds that might be bad for us. Our sources say he's got some kinda incriminatin' evidence stashed, the kind that might find its way to the DA even if he was dead. Yeah, but likewise, we don't want our friend to go into a more permanent retirement 'cause quite frankly we're hoping to reactivate him at some point. You know, on a specialty basis, somethin' like you, Mr. Phillips. Craftsmen is hard to come by. Lot of 'em in jail these days. Speaking of which, what happened to Fest?"

"Bifulco took care of it, just like old times, you might say. And it seems Smonig and Bifulco have decided to forget the whole thing."

"Heh-heh." There was only morbid satisfaction in the chuckles. "Just like ol' times. Where are they now, what's the picture?"

"They went fishing."

Silence on the other end. A car started, an air compressor rattled to a stop.

"Look out for our friend, Mr. Phillips, look out for our friend. I guess one way to work it would be t'eliminate this guy Smonig, but that might get the cops on Sid's case. I mean, he's a convicted murderer, an' livin' right next door. Another way to look at it, if Smonig somehow, like, finds out Sid is the guy that did his wife, he may be very pissed with our boy Bifulco. It's your call, Mr. Phillips, but for now maybe you better just try'n figure out exactly what Smonig knows while playin' guardian angel for Sid. See Smonig don't send Bifulco to sleep with the fishes." The line went dead.

When Omer turned away from the phone, he found the crow perched on his gearshift knob, pecking at loose change in the car's ashtray. The crow flapped madly, dropped a few feathers, and made for the sky, something silver gleaming in its beak.

Omer took off his crusher and played with the brim as he searched the sky for the thief.

"A delicate matter indeed."

Hands on her hips, Val shook her head at Little Bob, who lay sprawled on the couch before a snow-filled TV screen. He knew better than to try to bed down with the missus when he came in late. That just got him a lecture, especially on a Sunday.

Tapes were scattered about the VCR, camcorder open and empty nearby. Val sniffed derisively when she confronted the clutter. Why couldn't they have a DVD player like most people? Over at the Show Time Videomat the selection of VHS tapes was getting smaller and smaller. Her sister in Pittsburgh said that they don't even rent VHS format at all anymore where she lives. And then Bob had to buy that silly VHS camcorder at a tag sale.

White go-to-meeting gloves in hand, she singled out the rental boxes for *Reverend Jim Chattanooga's Jesus Jamboree* and *The Elvis Conspiracy*. Then she initiated the search for the tapes. One was on the floor. Oh—and the other tape she'd left in the machine. She'd fallen asleep in front of the TV waiting for Bob, and had finally dragged herself off to the bedroom around three a.m., a lecture fermenting in her mind. Training the evil eye on her prone hubby, she stuffed the tape one way, then the other into the tape box. Darned if she could remember which way they were supposed to go in.

Besides, she was in a hurry. She wanted to drop the tapes off at the Videomat "Nite Deposit" before church.

At the screen door, she stabbed sleeping Bob with a last reproachful glare. Wouldn't *he* feel guilty for having missed services.

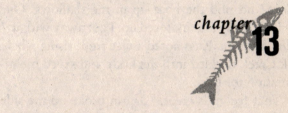

chapter **13**

"How much this tub set you back, Smonig?" Sid admired all Russ's gadgets—the sonar, rod holders, can holders, aerated baitwell—as they motored up-river toward the Eddy. "Yeah, 'cause I can't stay with that rowboat, gotta think about tradin' up."

"Ten or twelve thousand to replace it."

Two kingfishers zigged across the river, chattering and laughing.

"Twelve, huh? I may have to make a little investment. So where we goin'?"

"Just above the Eddy there's some rapids. Above the rapids is a stretch of water five feet deep bank to bank, water that really moves, and a field of small boulders. We anchor, fish, lift anchor, move up, drop anchor, fish, and so on. The larger bass hang right at the edge of the fastest, deepest water." Russ throttled back the motor as they arched into the Eddy. Rapids came into view. A washing-machine effect was at work through the center of the rapids.

"Whoa." Sid came to attention. "How're you gonna get through all that? Looks pretty rough."

"Up the right side. It's a little tricky. I used to go ashore and pull the boat up in the shallows. One day I felt lucky and motored up. I got away with it." In the distance, Russ noted a nice trout rising where Pink Creek trickled into the Eddy and saved the information for later.

"That feelin' is great." A grin broke up the side of Sid's face. "Gettin' away with somethin' like that, I mean."

"I guess you'd know a lot about that."

"I guess I would." Sid's grin broke into a smile. "But make no mistake, Russ. The only thing I wanna get away with now is bass, walleye, trout, muskellunge, those watchamacallits—the rocket-fish."

"Rocket-fish?"

"Yeah." Sid snapped a finger at Russ. "Shad."

"Shad. Well, you've come at a good time for them. Looked like the one you brought over the other night gave you quite a fight."

"Very amusing, Smonig. So how come I never heard of these here shad before I came here?"

"Sid, let me ask you something. I mean, I saw you casting, and you seem to have done a lot of it. You have a lot of tackle, and of the right kinds. You seem to know a lot about fish, but...is this the first time you've ever actually fished?"

"Smonig, to quote a certain deputy warden I once knew, the only fish in prison is on a bun with tartar sauce."

The bow swung to the right and over a burst of current and waves. The motor complained, and the blade whined and growled as it popped free of the water.

"You don't mean to tell me you learned to fish in prison?" He tilted back his fedora.

"I had a special program, got all the magazines, catalogs. The Warden, he's an outdoorsman. Gave me some pointers."

Scraping the bow briefly off a rock to the port side, Russ cut the boat through a swell that sent about ten gallons over the gunnels. But that was the end of the rapids. The boat moved into the slick headwater. They didn't go far before Russ pushed a toggle and the anchor motor fed cable. Soon they were stuck fast to the bottom. He flicked another switch, and a bilge pump started returning the ten gallons to the Delaware.

Russ produced a plastic compartmentalized tray full of squiggly-tailed rubber grubs, hooks, and attachments. "Take your pick of color, but with sun on the water I like the dark ones with sparkles."

Sid picked one, and while he was tying it on, Russ made his first cast. He was retrieving the cast in sharp jerks when—bang!—his rod was bent and pumping. A golden brown fish roughly the dimensions of a large baking potato arched out of the water and bore under the boat.

Sid cast, his grub plopping upriver in the folds of current.

"Whoa!" Sid hauled back, rod bent, vibrating, pumping. "Whoa, I got a friggin' fish!"

Sid looked briefly away from his battle. Russ was raising his rod again, the foot-long bass gasping. The jaws broke the surface. Russ's thumb and forefinger clamped onto the lower lip. He lofted the red-eyed fish by its lower jaw, the fins slowly fanning the air.

Sid held his rod high as his fish raced upstream. The bass's bronze sides flashed in the water. It bolted to sunlight and the surface, breaking free of the river. The fish pirouetted and spat Sid's grub at the boat. Splash and flicker: the bass was gone.

"Aw, crap." Sid stood motionless. "What was that? I had him. What was that?" He waved a hand toward where the fish went, arguing with it.

Russ unhooked his fish and placed it in the water. It thrashed from his grip, vanishing.

"That often happens when a fish jumps."

"What'd I do wrong?"

"When you feel them shoot for the surface, reel up and put your rod tip down. That discourages them from jumping. It also helps to keep a taut line if they do jump. Once the line is slack, they can shake the hook loose. But by the same token, you don't want to pull when they jump either."

"Huh." Sid smiled to himself. "So what you're sayin' is I gotta finesse the fish, that right?"

"Well, yeah, I guess you could say that." Russ hadn't thought of it until then, but Sid seemed to be full of finesse. "I'm sure you'll finesse the next one."

chapter **14**

It was only as Trooper Price lay on the ground bleeding that he'd suddenly remembered: Martha hadn't been wearing a bra. Hell, that's why he'd gone ape over her to begin with.

To say the least, his relief had been mixed. He'd only dodged one bullet. The other was in his chest.

X-rays and a little probing had shown that after the slug had passed through Price's citation folder, it entered his chest, cracked, and deflected off a rib. What remained of the hollow-point slug was tucked up under the next rib. He had been lucky. Very lucky.

He had a dime-sized hole two and a half inches below his nipple and a bruised area surrounding that. After plucking out the lead, the doctor stitched it up, slapped a Band-Aid on it, and gave him some antibiotics. He was sent home.

Price felt gypped.

If a cop gets shot in the chest and survives, he can usually expect a month off at the least. And who knows? Maybe he can get a sweet disability deal. A trooper Price knew slammed a cruiser door on his hand and suffered "permanent damage" to his trigger/pen finger. The digit in question had a fractured knuckle and had lost sixty percent of its mobility. So this guy gets an early retirement—way early—with eighty percent of his pay. Price had seen the guy recently, and his finger apparently had regained ninety-nine percent mobility. He was bowling with it. The ex-trooper was sitting pretty.

But Price didn't slam a door on his finger, he got shot in the chest. And what happens? Nothing. His injury was termed a "flesh wound," which meant he wasn't eligible for any of the bennies.

Now it was Sunday afternoon, and Price was planted in front of the TV. He was off duty, so he'd put the small diamond stud earring in his right ear. It was a vestige of something cool he and the guys in high school all did, and made him feel virile. His wife, Debbie—after setting him up with a beer, the channel changer, and a kiss—had run off to her sister's to gab. Even Debbie was acting like getting shot in the chest was no big deal.

So he sat there in his den, surrounded by all his high school football trophies, sipping beer, watching *The Sons of Katie Elder*, and wishing he'd gotten shot in the right index finger. That's when he decided that maybe he should pop in a tape. He didn't much feel in the mood for any of his Super Bowl tapes, much less any of the blooper tapes, much less *North Dallas Forty* or *The Longest Yard*.

Next to the VCR was a bag from the video store with the movies Debbie had picked up on her way home from shopping. One tape was some romantic comedy featuring that ugly French guy with greasy hair. Price loathed that stuff at any time. The other tape was *The Elvis Conspiracy*. Well, that's what the box said, but what was inside didn't look like a commercial tape. Probably a bootleg. It wasn't even rewound.

Price fed the tape into the machine.

Val chewed out Little Bob but good when she found him still asleep at noon. Godless wastrel that he was, Bob knew there would be no peace until he atoned. Some arduous yard work, followed by a visit to his mother-in-law's to clean the dog poop off her lawn, usually bought the Lord's forgiveness.

So it was after cleaning the gutters, shutters, and car, after weed-whacking the fence line, after scraping the BBQ grill and heading over to Mother's for tea and dog poo that Val took up her knitting and left Bob in peace late that Sunday afternoon. And as Val took a dim view of feasting on "God's Day," dinner was a cold sup of the individual's choosing, eaten apart. Bob had the whole rest of the day to himself. And, as was his way, he fell upon his camcorder.

It wasn't until he did so that he had a chance to really mull over the previous night's doings, which he'd reflected on from time to time throughout his chores. His general reaction was more awe over a character like Sid Bifulco than concern over the manslaughter cover-up.

Mechanically, Bob fumbled with the clutter of tapes, putting them back in their respective boxes. He recalled how well the whole evening had come out on tape, including all that stuff by the headlights with all that radiator steam. Especially since at the time he hadn't been aware the thing was taping. Those blank SUPER*PROCAM tapes he'd gotten at Wal-Mart held up well in low light. He'd watched the whole thing when he'd reached home the night before and had only fallen asleep sometime during Sid's "getting away with murder" speech.

Holding the last empty SUPER*PROCAM tape box in one hand and the last boxless tape, *The Elvis Conspiracy*, in the other, Bob suddenly realized something was amiss.

It took another fifteen minutes or so for him to realize the possible ramifications.

"Just walk him around the boat! Like a dog on a short leash!" Net poised for action, Russ jockeyed behind Sid.

"If this thing's a dog, it's a Doberman, Smonig—whoa!" Rod doubling, Sid lurched forward to keep the line from breaking.

"He's hiding under the boat. Just let him stay there a second. Keep the pressure on!"

"You said to let him sit there! So I'm lettin' him sit there!"

"O.K., sorry, just making sure you don't give any slack line." Russ backed off and took a deep breath. "When he comes out take him for another walk around the boat, then we'll see if we can bring him up for the net. Now, Sid, we don't want to net him at the front of the boat. There's not room for both of us there. And in back, there's a chance we'll foul the line in the propeller. Just pick a side, and you tell me when he's ready, O.K.?"

"How the hell will I know when he's ready? You think maybe I should ask the Doberman to roll over an' play dead? Oh crap, here he goes—here he goes...." The tip of the rod made two deep dips. The line buzzed off the reel. Russ stepped forward.

"I think this is it—his last run to the deep water. Reel up. You'll feel his head turn as he starts to come up."

"Hey—here he comes!"

"It's O.K."

"Here he comes...."

"Steady now, steady..."

"Ooh, there he is! Nab him, Smonig!"

"Not yet. Wait till he turns on his side. He may have one bolt left—a short one—be ready."

"Now, Smonig!"

"Wait—there he goes!"

"Whoa!"

More line buzzed off the reel. A tail splashed river water in their faces.

"O.K., Sid, bring him back, fast and headfirst and into the net." Russ plunged the green mesh hoop into the river.

"He's comin'!"

"Got him." Russ heaved the net aboard and stumbled backward—the boat tipped—Sid took an abrupt step backward and the seat cut his calves out from under him.

Man overboard.

Man down rapids.

Before he even clambered aboard, Sid was posing the usual question.

"How big?" He was dog-paddling smack in the middle of Hellbender Eddy like he spent every afternoon splashing about in the river. Well, truth be told, he had.

"Big. Maybe twenty-five. Maybe more." Russ held out a hand and Sid waved it off, draping one arm, then the other, then a leg over the gunnel. Sid went splat on the boat's wet carpet.

"Twenty-five pounds! Shit, that's gotta be some kinda record!" He ran his hands over his wet hair and pulled a grin up one side of his face.

"You may be right. On six-pound test line, I'd

say you may have a line-test record for the state of Pennsylvania." Russ produced a towel and a flask of whisky from a compartment under his seat. It wasn't the first time a sport had taken a plunge.

"Pennsylvania? Hell, the whole goddamn country! The world! I never seen a record of a smallmouth bass that big! What's the face for, Smonig?"

Russ hauled the subdued fish from the livewell and laid it between them. The girthsome copper fish gasped and his eyes goggled; he looked like a mondo goldfish.

"Don't tell me that's not the biggest goddamn smallmouth you ever saw, Smonig!" Sid shook his towel at the big bronze monster. It was the kind of whopper whose size was truly indicated by extended arms and the phrase "He was this big!"

"Sid, this is not a smallmouth. It's a carp."

"A carp?"

"That's right. A carp, a very big carp." Russ was trying his best to sound upbeat. Fair or not, "game fish" is a label less likely to be associated with carp than "trash fish" or, as in this case, "booby prize."

"So why the sour puss, Smonig? You look like you just lost a filling."

Russ started the motor and turned the boat downriver.

"I guess I was hoping it was a muskellunge, that's all." Russ shrugged.

Sid took a pull from the flask and shook his head.

"Don't rush me, Smonig. Look, I been at this

three days. I got one rocket-fish, fifteen smallmouth, and one carp that's big enough to bury in a coffin. What do you want from me?"

"You're right—I'm sorry. And just as soon as we get in, we'll rush this thing—I mean this carp—over to the grocer, weigh it, sign an affidavit, take a photo, then release it."

"Smonig, is this a trophy fish or what? It's a record, am I right?" They stared at each other a moment, the boat had navigated the rapids and was buzzing around the bend below the Eddy, the sun just dipping behind Little Hound Mountain.

"Taxidermist?" Russ ventured.

"Ab-so-lutely," Sid agreed.

Amber sunlight drew long shadows from the trees, and the purple sky cleared of all clouds. Buds along the stream bank, while barely noticeable that morning, were now bursting like popcorn. Two kingfishers brattled and swooped toward their New York bank, and the trout sipped tiny gray mayflies at Pink Creek. A blue heron stalked the shallows for tadpoles. Considering the way the day had started—at night, in the steam and glare on the driveway—things seemed to have improved dramatically. And even as Russ had tried throughout the day to touch on the frightening implications of all that had happened, he seemed unable to focus on it, as though it were a fading dream he soon wouldn't remember at all.

Where was the body? Would anybody find it? Would Russ go to jail for manslaughter? Hit-and-run driving? Either he was incapable or his mind was unwilling to bear down on these issues. After all, he was fishing, and as much as it was his profession, he did enjoy it. Especially on a sunny day in which the bass hit all day long. And Russ was, after all, a pushover for the triumphant neophyte, having been one himself. Awash in denial and distraction, Russ bounced the boat around a bend and toward his landing.

"Hey, Smonig, who is that Trout Lady anyhow? She live around here?"

Russ smiled at the moniker.

"The Trout Lady's name is Jenny Baker. She lives north of the Eddy with her brother Matt in a trailer. Why, you thinking of..."

"Yeah, I thought I might. She seems about my speed."

"That she is, Sid, that she is." Russ's smile vanished when he spied Big and Little Bob standing at the landing.

Little Bob was pacing, and he didn't have his camcorder with him. Russ sensed trouble.

Sid registered Russ's mood swing and looked to shore.

"Hey, whadda these guys want now? Jeez. Hey, Russ. Russ!" Sid waved a hand, and Russ lapsed into his tired look. "Hey, relax, everything's O.K. Trust me, things'll be fine."

"You filmed what? A video store? C'mere...no, right here, and tell me that again." Sid was waving

Little Bob over to where he stood, but the latter kept pacing and staring at the ground.

"It was an accident! I didn't know the camera was on, then my wife put the SUPER*PROCAM tape in *The Elvis Conspiracy* box and returned it to the video store and now I'm afraid to try an' get it back 'cause they might recognize me if they watched the tape. And the police! The police might be there right now, waiting, staking out the video store. I'm so sorry! It's like so impossible, I dunno how it coulda happened . . . it's just impossible!"

"Yo, Big Guy, grab the Little Guy and bring him over here."

Big Bob knitted a brow and stood his ground.

"Hey look, Big Guy, I ain't gonna hurt him. He's hysterical, and one thing we gotta do is keep our heads. Am I right?"

Big Bob conceded the point with a shrug. He clamped Little Bob's shoulders between two hands, lifted him, and placed him in front of Sid.

"What's his name?" Sid snapped his fingers at Big Bob.

"Bob Cropsey, but most people call him Little Bob."

"Sure. O.K. Yo, Bobby, look at me. Look at me, Bobby, everything's O.K. Now just tell me: where is this video store?"

"Down the road." Little Bob's lip was atremble, and he sniffed back tears.

"Do you know how to get there?"

"I guess, yeah."

"Good." Sid clapped his hands. "Our problems are solved."

"How do you figure, Sid?" Russ's voice was eerily monotone, his face blanched. "None of us can go in there. Like he said, we're all on the tape. If they've seen it, we'll be recognized. I dunno about you guys, but I think we should tell the police exactly—"

"Tell them exactly what, Smonig? That you killed somebody while driving around in the bag?"

Russ's face went from white to red.

"Yes."

"O.K., so who did you kill, tell me that?"

Big Bob spoke up.

"You said it was some guy named—"

"Wrong." Sid pointed a finger in Big Bob's face. "The who in this case is a what, and where is that what? You don't know, I don't know."

"How could you not know?" Russ blurted.

"Look, you guys wanna go to the cops, tell 'em Russ killed a guy, and that you two are accessories, and then not have a fish to show 'em?" Sid threw his arms out. "You guys'll look pretty friggin' stupid, to be honest."

"But you took the . . ." Russ began.

"What did I do? Did you see me do anything? O.K., O.K., say we all go to court. You say you killed somebody and then 'cause I'm some kinda saint, I came in and ditched the stiff for you. You know what my defense attorney is gonna say to you? 'Mr.

Smonig, did you actually see the defendant dispose of the body? Did you see the defendant single-handedly lift a guy who's gotta be two hundred an' eighty pounds, throw him in the car, and drive him to points unknown?' Then he'll ask your two friends. And the answer will be no. N-O. Now see, you're gonna look pretty foolish. Not that any of this is goin' to court anyhow 'cause this here is circumstantial, and for another thing, there ain't no body. Spanky? Alfalfa? Porky? Is any of this gettin' through? Do you know what I'm talkin' about? And do you get what it means? Two words. Are you listening? Two words: Don't Panic." Sid smiled, clapped his hands, and headed for the dam breast and his cabin.

"Hey, where are ya going? What are we gonna do?" Big Bob beseeched, waving his arms.

"What're we gonna do? We're gonna call a taxidermist, and then we're all gonna go get that tape."

"We can't. Today's Sunday. They're closed at four on Sundays. Nobody'll be there," Little Bob moaned.

"Hey, if there was someone there then there'd be somebody to recognize us. Am I right? Hey, it's perfect. We break in and grab the tape. I'll pick you guys up in five minutes."

Sid disappeared behind the willow.

After viewing the tape twice, Price had the video freeze-frame on the dim, flickery image of Johnny Fest's face, eyes open, mouth open, looking just a little surprised and quite dead. Sure, the tape quality was poor in the low light under the truck, and the camera sat at a weird angle.

But Price knew that face. O.K., so he had focused more on lost disability opportunities than on the trauma of being shot. It had been pretty hairy though, and if he'd had any time to consider his predicament before the gun went off, it would have been downright disturbing. But Price was a former gridiron champ and had an instinctively cool reaction to injury. And the whole thing had happened damned fast.

However, it hadn't happened so fast that the face of the guy behind the trigger didn't stick. Hell, there was no question that the guy flickering on the screen was the guy who shot him. The red and white striped shirt clearly visible under the back of the truck made it a positive I.D. And with what all these people on the tape were saying, well, it got Price to thinking. He phoned the barracks.

"Stoney?... Hey, it's Price.... No, I'm O.K., fine, yeah, really.... Oh, it just glanced off a rib.... Yeah, a hollow point. Look, Stoney, is there a make on the guy that...yeah...Johnny Fest, huh...yeah... Anybody grab him?... Yeah, from the composite?... What?... Uh-huh. Newark?... Whoa, the guard's eyes... You're shitting me, no kidding?... You're damned right I feel lucky.... What?... A reward? Who?...oh, the Brotherhood of Guards, huh?... No—really? You're joking. Is that legal?... But doesn't that really mean 'Dead or Alive?'... Yeah, well, that's what I thought.... Yeah, I guess they all would be out hoping to find that BMW... Uh-huh, look, Stoney, I gotta go.... Yeah, Monday... Right. I will, yeah.... O.K.... Yes, bye."

Price slammed the phone down and turned to the TV screen. He tugged absently at his diamond stud earring, contemplating his options.

"I might just cash in on this thing after all."

Price winked at the TV and finished his flat beer. He burped, blinked off the VCR, got his windbreaker, and left the house.

The sky had gone scarlet mackerel, and the day was drawing to an appropriately lusty close.

Chik was showing Penelope the storyboard for his next "tour de force" when Omer came into the Five Star and nobly doffed his hat to the lady.

Slapping the binder closed, Chik stashed the dirty opus *Rubber Bikini Bingo* under the counter, smoothed his mustache, and approached his customer. Penelope seemed to have a tune in her head. She swayed to the music, sucking cola from a straw.

"Tea with lemon coming right up," Chik chimed.

"My, what a keen memory you have." Omer tore his gaze from Penelope. She was a dead ringer for a naughty little number he'd whisked away from the Naval Observatory one night in the midst of one of Washington's worst snowstorms.

Chik clinked the tea in front of Omer.

"Haven't seen Mr. Big and Sweaty," Chik apologized.

"Well"—Omer tossed a cursory glance at Penelope, who clearly wasn't paying any attention—"there's somebody else I'm looking for. Have you seen Sid around? Lately?"

Chik massaged a hand towel and thought.

"Yeah, he stopped in last night. First time I met him. Came in looking for Russ. I told him he might find him down at the Duck Pond."

"That tavern down the road? I see. Have you seen either Russ or Sid today?" Omer sipped his tea, pinky extended.

"Nope. But I do know this much: Russ and Sid was fishing, and this guy Sid came up with some kinda huge carp. Our local taxidermist was in, sayin' he was gonna drop over later tonight to pick it up on his way back from an auction in Honesdale. Can you imagine? Mounting a carp?" Chik rolled the dishrag between two hands. He was hoping for another of Omer's twenties.

"Any idea"—Omer paused to sip tea—"where I might find them now?"

"Nope. But I'll keep an eye out. Hey, if there's a number I can call or something..."

The front door opened and a cop stepped in. Not that he was in uniform or anything. He was a tall, formerly lean man in blue Dickies and a baby blue windbreaker over a bowling shirt. The blond hair was more or less cut into a flattop.

Both Chik and Omer had been around long

enough to know a cop if he was wearing a raccoon coat, Indian headdress, and elf shoes. Or even a diamond stud earring.

Price took in his surroundings, hands on hips, before finally stepping up to the counter next to Omer. Price started to fold his arms, but realized that would hurt his bullet wound. Instead, he let his arms hang, though a bit restlessly.

"What can I get you—mister?" Chik was a little tense.

Price knitted his brow. How did people always know he was a cop?

"Yes, I'm looking for a friend of mine." Price smiled unconvincingly. "I was just passing through, thought I'd look him up." He smiled harder, and it didn't help. "My friend's name is Sid." He glanced at Penelope as she vapidly vacuumed the last of the cola in a protracted slurp. "Do you know where I might find him?"

Chik tried not to glance at Omer, who was examining his nails.

"Can't say I have seen your friend. That is, I don't know him, haven't heard of him, really." Chik was twisting his rag.

Omer piped up.

"Isn't that the guy who lives down by . . . ? No, that's Fred Primely." Omer put a hand on Price's forearm, noting the name "Price" embroidered on the cop's bowling shirt. "What a weird character Fred is. Let me tell you. Why, he has a three-legged

dog, a two-legged cat, and a one-legged bird."
Omer knew how to scare snoops off: drivel.

"But you don't know Sid Bifulco?" Price went
back to arms akimbo. He didn't like people touching him and didn't want to invite more of Omer's
friendly pats.

"Well, let me see," Omer began, "there's this lady
over in Milford. Her name is Syd—that's short for
Sydney, like in Australia. Did you know that was a
girl's name? Well I didn't, not 'til..."

Price slid over to Penelope, who had her back
and elbows against the counter. She looked up at
Price from under a dark chocolatey forelock. He
could see she wasn't wearing a bra, and he forced
that thought from his mind.

"Excuse me, ma'am, I was just asking those gen-
tlemen whether they knew where I might find a
friend of mine that lives around here. His name is
Sid." There was that awful smile of his again, like he
was peddling stale bread.

Penelope sloshed a languid glance in Chik's direction, but the latter didn't move a muscle. Despite
the girl's distracted Veronica Lake demeanor, she
wasn't as vapid as some assumed. She shook her
head and shrugged.

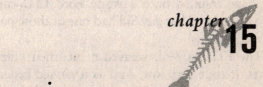

chapter

15

Jenny worked most weekends, because a day's pay was as hard to turn down as a round on the house. So she had spent Sunday afternoon making delivery of eight hundred ten- and fourteen-inch brown trout to some hoity-toity private club down off I-84 called simply "The Meadows." Anyhow, they tipped well and they didn't insist she put the trout in buckets. They didn't even count them, which meant that Jenny could just back the truck down the boat ramp and blow the entire contents of each tank. Which was nice, because then she didn't have to haul water around looking for a place to surreptitiously dump it. People get real upright when they see a tank truck, even if it's just carrying fishy water, dumping willy-nilly. And most places she delivered to didn't want the "dirty" trout-farm water in their lake.

It was about eight p.m., dark and misty. Jenny was sitting in her truck at the shopping center across from Little Tony's, eating pizza, listening to the country station, staring blankly across the way at all the closed shops, and thinking idly about that weird airline pilot guy, Sid, standing in a tree in his bathrobe. Then, as if she'd worked some bizarre spell, her gaze zoomed onto a white Ford LTD coming across the lot. That guy Sid had one of those parked in his driveway.

The LTD slowed, weaved a bit, then killed its lights. It rode very low. And as it passed beneath a streetlamp, Jenny registered two faces behind the glass, one in the front passenger seat, one in the back. Arching away from her, the car headed down past the last dark shop on the row, the Show Time Videomat, and disappeared behind.

Mid-chew, Jenny struggled to swallow a chunky bit of crust. The two faces were not just familiar, they were Russ and Big Bob. In Sid's car.

The brilliant day had given way to a humid night. Down by the river it would be chilly. But the tarmac of the strip mall's parking lot retained heat and gave off water vapor that made light from the lampposts look like beacons from a submersible.

Sid had used a Dumpster behind the Videomat to hike himself up onto the roof. His comrades stood below, looking up at his silhouette.

"Now look, Sid, we are just after the tape, right?

I mean, we're not making off with any money, and there aren't going to be any alarms going off, police, that sort of thing?" Russ was literally wringing his hands, searching the surroundings for the FBI.

Sid ignored him.

"You see, the best way to break in just about anywhere is through someplace on the roof. A hatch, a skylight, a vent hood, something like that is usually much easier to open than any door, and usually not rigged to an alarm." Sid threw his hands up as if to show how easy it was.

"Back up a second there. What do you mean 'not usually rigged' with an alarm? Sid, how will you know?" Russ protested.

"Big Bobby, what's with your friend here? I don't think he has confidence in me. No confidence in the guy who's led a life of crime."

"And who—incidentally—got caught," Russ added.

"Now, don't you guys think that if I can get away with all that over a twenty-year period that I can get away with breaking in to a Podunk video store in ten minutes? You're damn right I can." Turning from his audience, he took a few steps onto the center of the roof and scanned his surroundings. Except for a drain riser coming up from the bathroom, it looked to be completely featureless, gravel-covered tar.

"Crap. It ain't gonna be easy," Sid muttered to himself, brandishing a pry bar. In his youth, all the old buildings of Newark had skylights, stairwells, ventilation shafts, and hatches. Warehouses and restaurants had big vent hoods. But he was unaware of the vagaries of shopping center architecture. The place probably had no basement either, the next best place for forced entry.

After inspecting the six-inch diameter riser, tugging on it, and kicking gravel around looking for the outline of a hatch, Sid was on the verge of admitting that they might have to go through the door after all. Then he heard the growl of an approaching truck. Sid crouched and listened as the slow grumbling truck curved around the side of the store. Air brakes sighed back near the LTD, a door opened and closed. Something banged the top of the Dumpster.

"Sid!" came a hoarse whisper.

He crept over to the edge and knelt.

"Hey, it's Trout Lady. Whadda you doin' here? You know, I didn't exactly send out invitations."

"Sid, are ya airline pilots always hanging out up on high places?" Arms folded, Jenny stood on the Dumpster and considered Sid's silhouette, her lips in a sardonic twist.

"I dunno who keeps spreading it aroun' that I'm like some kinda airline pilot."

"It's me, flyboy. Say, just what are ya doin' up there anyways?"

"Me?" Sid gestured at his chest.

"Yeah, you. And where are the Bobs and Russ?" Jenny craned her neck, trying to see behind neighboring Dumpsters.

Sid took a cursory look and shrugged it off.

"I dunno. They were around here someplace. You musta scared 'em into ditching. Hey, what are *you* doing here anyways? Where'd you come from?"

"O.K., I'll go first. I was comin' back from a delivery down off I-84, stopped in for pizza at Little Tony's. Was out in my truck eating a slice when I saw your car come by with Russ and Big Bob's face in it. I don't know for a fact that Little Bob is here, but where ya find one, ya often find the other. Now it's your turn."

"What do you think I'm doing here?" Sid flashed a lopsided grin.

"Well, I don't think you're an airline pilot at all. I think you're a crook."

"A crook? Hey, you got it all wrong. You wanna know what a crook is? That's like a politician, a judge, or government-type guy that takes graft. That's what a crook is. But me? No, I'm not a crook. A burglar? O.K., so tonight I'm a burglar. But just to help some friends in a jam, God in the witness stand." Sid crossed himself as though he were still Catholic. Though he'd never received notice from the Vatican, he took it for granted he'd been excommunicated.

"An' you're gonna break in to this here video store from the roof? To help some friends? Meaning the Bobs and Russ? And for no, as they say, 'personal gain'?"

Sid pointed and nodded at each of her questions in turn.

"But I'll tell you the truth. I do have a personal

agenda—to be honest." He held up a pledging palm.

"Ya do?"

"Yup." Sid looked around, his voice lowering further. "Y'see, if I help Russ outta this jam, I'm gonna get in on all his hot fishing spots."

"No shit!"

"Yeah shit!" Sid sounded defensive.

"What about his secret shad spots?" Jenny leaned one leather-jacketed shoulder against the brick wall, whispering up at Sid in a conspiratorial tone.

"Those slices and the rest of the pie!" Sid winked.

"Hey, Sid, I got an idea. Actually, it's a deal."

"A deal?"

"Yeah. Look. What if I turn ya all into the police..."

"Stop right there. Do you mean to say you'd rat out the Bobs and Russ?"

"And ya, to the cops. What do ya think?"

"No way. You wouldn't do that."

"O.K., maybe I wouldn't. But how about this: How about I show ya how to get in here? That, plus I keep a lid on this burglary—*plus* that Russ has got some kinda big problem—which would only get worse if everybody knew something was up, whatever it is—all in exchange for ya showin' me Russ's spots." Jenny let that sink in a minute. "Especially the shad spots."

"O.K., how about this," Sid countered shrewdly.

"I personally will take you to each spot he shows me for an afternoon's fishing, not to exceed five spots, and I'll take you out to dinner somewhere nice around here."

"Dinner? Who said anything about dinner?"

"I did. Hey, if you want, I'll even take you to Little Tony's, but if I was you I'd go for the big money, like someplace French. Then maybe you could put on a dress, some nice, uh, shoes maybe. I'll even wear a tie."

"Ya wanna take the Trout Lady on a date?"

"Whadda I gotta do, Jenny? Spell it out on a pizza in pepperoni?"

"Shhh, dammit! Get down off that roof, Sid. Ya gotta deal."

Ten minutes later, after the Bobs and Russ had crawled sheepishly out of the shrubbery, and after they'd moved the LTD and truck back around front, Jenny instructed them all to retreat into the forest shadow behind the video store.

"Jenny, this better not be one of your jokes!" Russ fished around the bushes for the fedora a twig had removed from his head.

"Hey, ya owe me that shad spot, Russ. Any more of your lip an' I'll up it to two or three." Jenny pointed at the rustling bushes. "Now ya guys settle down. Be real quiet, an' watch the master at work. Used to get beer like this." Jenny marched up to the back of the video store.

Crushing his fedora back on his head, Russ grabbed Sid by the shirtsleeve.

"What the hell did you bring her in on this for! What did you tell her?"

"Relax. I didn't tell her nothin', Smonig. All she knows is that we're in some kinda jam. I cut a deal with her." Sid shrugged off Russ's grip.

"Deal? Deal? What kind of deal?"

"Would you stop clawing at my goddamn shirt, Smonig. Relax! What, you think I promised her something? O.K., I promised her dinner, Smonig. You can get almost anything outta a lady with an expensive dinner."

"Y'guys! Shut up!" Jenny stood in front of the back door, gauged her distance, then ran toward it. A red hiking boot rose to the occasion and kicked the bottom of the door. The impact echoed down the alleyway, but the door remained closed. Jenny disappeared between the Dumpster and the wall.

Some time passed, and the gang in the bushes fought off itches, aches, and sneezes. Eyes strained to cut through the shadows and make out fuzzy dark images of the brickwork and door frame.

Kicking the back door was not intended to open it. The idea was to move it just enough to break the circuit on a magnetic sensor, thus triggering a silent alarm. Back when she had worked hauling Pepsi in Hawley, a beer-hound they'd called Whiz used to get into the beer distributor at Indian Orchard in just such a fashion, whence he would liberate a few cases of Yuengling.

Sure enough, headlights flashed the bushes, and a white late-model Chevy with an eagle emblem on each door swept up behind the store and screeched to a stop. High beams flicked on, fully illuminating the back door to the store. More time passed as the security guy sat in his car considering the possibility that it was a false alarm.

Finally, the girthsome guard groaned out of the sedan and sputtered something unintelligible into a walkie-talkie. Producing a ten-pound ring of keys, he counted them off and jammed one into the lock of the back door. Shouldering the door open, he scanned the shop interior with a log-sized flashlight. He went in, leaving the door ajar.

Jenny slid from behind the Dumpster and peeked inside. She crept farther and farther until she was gone.

"Hey, Jenny went in the store!" Little Bob squeaked.

"She's gonna get caught," Big Bob predicted.

"Boy, has she ever got nerve!" Little Bob countered.

"Ho—keep it down." Sid was familiar with Jenny's ploy, and he didn't like it much. A guard would normally start searching from the back of a store, an area usually full of hiding places in stored merchandise, and move toward the front of the store. Standard procedure so he won't get jumped by anybody. When finished, he would return to the back door without searching the spots he'd already searched—which was where Jenny would be hiding. The alarm control box is often next to the back door where curious customers don't have access to it, either physically or visually.

After probing the premises, the guard would re-set the alarm by punching in his access code. Jenny, meanwhile, would be watching the guard punch in his code and would be able to disarm it once he'd left.

Clever as it was, Sid didn't like it much, if for no other reason than that it seemed dishonest. An honest break-in involved forced entry. Oh well. Sid figured this wasn't one for the record anyhow.

Sure enough, no sooner had the guard left than Jenny was leaning in the open doorway.

"C'mon, fellahs. Let the crime wave begin!"

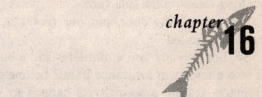

chapter **16**

The ride back to Hellbender Eddy was as festive as a fish fry in the rain. The tape wasn't in the video store. In fact, it looked like it had been rented out.

Big Bob broke the silence as they were coming down Ballard Road.

"Mechanic said your truck should be ready this week, Russ. Said he'd never seen anything like what happened to that steering box, locking up and busting like that."

As Sid turned the LTD down the driveway and the headlights swept across the Smonig abode, Russ flashed to the events of the previous night. The crunch, the thud, the steam. An icy spider of doom marched up his neck.

"Yeah, it's a pretty neat trick, but the cops buy into it. Makes for a perfect 'accident.' Especially when the cause of death is watchamacallits." Sid snapped his fingers. "Head drama."

Little Bob raised his hand.

"I think that's head *trauma,* Mr. Bifulco."

"What I said, head trauma."

The LTD ground to a stop at the Smonig trailer, headlights spotlighting the old powder blue Dodge sprouting weeds in the side yard.

Russ opened the door, put one foot out, then turned back to Sid.

"So, not only are you a murderer and a burglar, but also a master at insurance fraud? Let me guess, steering boxes are a specialty? I happen to know quite a lot about steering boxes, and anybody who knows anything about cars wouldn't buy it. And the police? They only know what the mobsters who pay them off let them think. Gangsters like you, probably. And you think it's some kinda game, but the innocent people who get in the way of your moves get chewed up."

"Whoa, Russ, whoa." The menace of Russ's stormy, cold stare and trembling voice surprised Sid.

"There's no 'whoa' about it. You love this stuff, dumping dead bodies, videotapes, ruin, prison: I'm on to you, Sid."

The door to the LTD slammed, and Russ stalked off toward his gloomy trailer. The gang in the car shared a silent moment.

"Hey, sure, so maybe Russ isn't all wrong. Gotta admit, this does seem a little like old times. But I swear to you guys—FBI as my judge—I'm not, and will not, drag this thing out. I'll, y'know, hit the video store tomorrow, get the tape during working hours when that guy in the store files—Price—returns it. Maybe nobody'll have looked at the whole thing. You said the beginning was long an' boring, am I right? I mean, there's this long bit while the camera is on the car seat?"

"Yeah, but I didn't rewind, I don't think." Little Bob sighed, dejected.

"I think I should go in and talk to Russ. I think he needs someone to talk to." Big Bob pushed the front seat forward, opened the door, and squeezed out.

"Big Bobby, if you ask me, kinda seems like Russ wants to be alone. Maybe you should try him to-morrow, know what I'm talkin' about? Y'guys go on home. Everything'll be awright."

Little Bob stepped out of the car too, and Big Bob held the door.

"I dunno." Big Bob scratched thoughtfully at his stubble, the car's dome light illuminating him up to the belt buckle. "Ya think maybe Russ is a little sui-cidal? There was a whole *Newstime* on that back in December. You gotta keep an eye on people under stress."

"Hey, whatever you wanna do, Big Guy. But I don't recommend it, know what I mean? See you guys around."

Sid threw the car in reverse and shot backward up the drive.

The Bobs decided to head home.

* * *

There was only one occasion when Sid had thought he was going to get whacked, and he'd left a mental bookmark at that page.

He'd been in with the Palfuttis maybe three years. Having sacked with a little number in fuchsia pumps, Sid was unable to tear himself away from his liaison for a weekly business meeting. It was the wrong thing to do, but he was young and a little cocky, so to speak. He showed up two hours late.

The Palfutti boardroom was a canyon of corrugated boxes surrounding a card table and four metal chairs in the A2Z Supermarket basement, and when Sid arrived late, it was deserted, lit only by a fluorescent bulb buzzing overhead. There was the usual smell of rotting lettuce and rat poison. Cigarette smoke still loitered in the air. When he turned to leave, placing a hand on the light switch, he somehow—either through some small sound made by a grin, the faintest whiff of macho musk, or the radiant body heat of a carnivore—realized he was not alone. Someone was there, hiding, waiting for him, ready to gut him.

Sid turned out the lights and left. The person never showed himself, even though there had been every opportunity to slit him. The intended message had come through loud and clear: Don't fuck up.

What was it with the red shoes? A curse? That incident had been preceded by fuchsia pumps. This time, Sid had just come from a tête-à-tête with Jenny and her crimson hikers. Warning lights flashed in

Sid's cerebral cortex as he stepped away from the LTD toward his front porch. He could feel eyes watching him from a dark recess. Someone was waiting in the shadows.

If it were a mob hit, the killer would show himself and do the work with a knife or wire because it was more brutal. They liked their rats to know they were getting whacked, and they liked to leave an ugly mess to discourage future rats. So if it were someone hiding around the side of the cabin, the assassin would have to rush up from behind while Sid was standing at the door. The hit would have been designed to make sure Sid suffered.

The steady churning rhythm of the river filled Sid's ears. His senses reached out, expanded, sharpened. Warm pine needles and cedar shingles choked his sinuses, the bug-light porch lamp stung his eyes, gravel crunched under his feet like shattering lightbulbs. A shovel leaning against the cabin, in the garden near the porch, drew his watering eyes. His palm stretched, ready to grasp.

Dead ahead, a man with a blond flattop and baby blue windbreaker stepped from behind the side of the cabin. Sid's vision swam—for an instant.

"I'm here about the fish." Trooper Price had been a little nervous about matching wits with a mobster of Sid's reputation, and had decided it would be best to try to sound tough and use mob jargon. When he'd stopped at the Duck Pond in his quest to find out where Sid lived, he'd had a drink or two and debated for a while whether to use the word "stiff" or "fish." Price stood in the amber light, hands flexing at his sides and his diamond stud a spark at his ear.

Sid waggled his shoulders, relaxing.

"Shit, you're here about the fish." Sid tapped his forehead. He'd forgotten: the taxidermist. A drop of sweat slid down his shirt collar.

"So you're not...surprised?" Price took a tentative step forward.

"Well, I guess a little. Didn't even see your car."

"Parked up the drive a little. I wanted it to be a surprise. Then you know why I'm here?"

"Yeah, you want the fish." Sid was looking through some keys for the one that opened the front door.

"I know all about how you and Russ whacked him." Price hunched his shoulders, trying to sneer.

"Yeah? Pretty exciting, huh? And he is a big mother, know what I'm talkin' about?" Sid propped the screen door open with one foot.

"I don't suppose you know about the reward?" Price rocked on his heels.

"Reward?" Sid pushed the door open. "C'mon in."

These mobsters sure were slick. Real cool. He followed cautiously.

"Yes, reward." Price took a look behind the door before entering.

"I didn't know they gave rewards. Shit, I'm sure glad I didn't chuck him in the river."

"Then you didn't dump him?"

"No way. The bastard's right here." Sid nudged

an oversized Styrofoam cooler with his foot. It was a florist's cooler, over four feet long and almost three feet wide, that had come loaded with flowers from Endelpo as a housewarming gift. Along with the carp, Sid had packed it full of ice and then generously duct-taped it closed.

Price looked at the giant cooler, confusion flickering on his face.

"In there?" Price went a little pale.

"Yeah, he was a monster, but I made him fit, know what I mean? Once you let the blood out they kinda deflate. But don't worry. I numbered all the pieces so you can, like, put him back together," Sid jested. He stuck his thumbs in his belt loops and gave Price a good-humored wink.

Denial was past, and Russ was faced with the fact that he'd killed a man. Who was he? Was there someone, a wife perhaps, waiting for a spouse that wasn't coming home? There seemed to be a terrible twist of fate at work.

But Russ hadn't gotten very far with this line of thought or his Yuengling before there was a knock at the door.

"Go away, Sid." Russ curled into a tighter knot on the couch.

There was a cough from beyond the door.

"It's not Sid."

"Go away."

"Mr. Smonig, I think I can help you."

Hairs stood up on Russ's neck.

When he opened the door, he didn't expect to see a little dark bow-tied gentleman with a wool crusher. And as Omer had been out in the chill from the river, his slightly pointed ears and cherubic cheeks had a radish hue.

"Well?" Russ slid the fedora back on his head and leaned a forearm on the door frame. "Who are you?"

Omer shook his head with concern, his brittle blue eyes inspecting Russ. He sighed.

"You know, Mr. Smonig, you're in a terrible mess, and I think you need all the help you can get! Now come along...."

Omer pushed past Russ and grabbed him by the hand.

"Hey, hey..." Russ protested.

Omer spun Russ into a chair at the kitchen table, grabbed his face in two delicate brown hands, and turned it to the light for inspection. The fedora was dispatched and Omer ran his fingers through Russ's hair.

"What you need is not beer, but tea."

In a flash, Omer had doffed his crusher and rolled up his sleeves.

Like an alligator whose tummy had been stroked, Russ snapped from his momentary trance.

"Who are you? What makes you think you can help me? Who told you I'm in trouble? Was it Jenny? Goddammit..."

Omer turned a pair of disapproving brown irises on Russ.

"We'll have no foul expletives, if you please, Mr. Smonig." Omer found a clean coffee cup in the cupboard, filled it with water, and produced an envelope of tea from his pocket. "Not only is it unbecoming, but distracting and full of negative energies. We must work toward a positive solution!"

"O.K., who the hell are you and what makes you think you can help me?"

Omer put the cup in the microwave and pressed a button. The oven hummed.

"The name is Phillips, and let's just say I overheard your exchange with Mr. Bifulco about the steering box. Good Lord, man—don't you think I know what you're up to?" Omer gave Russ a disappointed, fatherly wag of his head. "And for a man who has seen as much adversity and hardship as Russell Smonig, this predicament is what I unwaveringly refer to as trouble!"

"I want half the reward," Price blurted.

"What?"

"That's right, half." Price gave Sid a steely eye.

"The reward is how much?"

"Ten thousand smackers."

"Shit, you want five thousand to stuff that fish? What're you, outta your friggin' mind?"

Price assumed "stuff" was mob verbiage for "turn a blind eye" or "make go away."

"That's right. I don't see as how you have any choice."

"Why not?"

"Otherwise parties'll find out about you and the fish. People around here don't take kindly to that kind of thing, friend. Know what I mean?" Price snarled.

Sid squinted, patting the air with his hands, sure he was misunderstanding somehow. "What is this?"

"You think you can just walk in here and kill a fish? It doesn't work like that."

Sudden realization betrayed itself on Sid's face. Of course. How could he have been so stupid? That's why Russ was acting so funny about the carp in the boat. Sure, Sid had heard about bass tournaments, what with their $100,000 prizes. He'd also heard about the competitiveness, the cheating, and how some guy who ratted about some bass-planting actually had his head vaporized by a shotgun blast. Had Sid Bifulco, career hoodlum, been so naive as to think that things in the country would be different from Newark? Had he been so naive as to think that every corner of the planet wasn't loaded with rackets where the locals didn't exactly invite competition? It all made sense. That's why Jenny was so knocked out about getting a shad spot. She was just a broad in crimson hikers looking for the inside track and tangling him further in the rackets. Sid had foolishly believed these people fished for the fun of it. But fishing too was a racket, probably dressed up like a "contest" and with "rewards" for the payoff on long odds of big fish. It was like a numbers racket. Or something like that. His mind was swamped with all the possibilities.

At that moment, Sid began to seriously consider whether red shoes had anything directly to do with his foul-ups. Were they the disease or merely a symptom?

Price finally got the reaction he was looking for. Sid's offhand exterior began to fade.

"Hey, uh, let's say we siddown, have a drink..." Sid tugged distantly on one ear.

Sid figured everything would have been O.K. if he hadn't caught the big fish. And that's why Russ wasn't so thrilled about the big fish, because his mob captain was gonna think he tried to put the fix on the contest. He only hoped the Bobs weren't informers, or that the crew captain wouldn't find out Sid planned to divulge all the inside fishing dope to Jenny.

Pouring two tumblers of Canadian, Sid handed one to Price and sat on the edge of the sofa.

"I see you're beginning to get the picture now, aren't you?" Price's chest inflated.

Sid stared at the floor, mind consumed with potential organized crime constructs.

"O.K." Sid paused, setting his jaw. "So how do we go about the reward thing?"

"Don't go through with it. Let it go, Russell. There's no sense in it, believe me. I know." Omer sat on a kitchen chair with good posture, hands laced over one knee. Russ lay on the couch, hands folded on his chest like a good patient.

They spoke in round terms, which, of course, were apt to leave out all the hard edges, many of which were crucial to the specific matter at hand. Omer and the folks of Hellbender Eddy seemed to have developed a habit of miscommunication. He was fixed on Russ's wife's steering box, while his patient was focused on the International's steering box.

"How can I? I can't stop thinking about that tape!" Russ sighed, gulping some tea. He didn't like tea, but this stuff was somehow different.

"Tape?"

"Yes, yes. It's all on tape, and it's lost!" Russ draped a forearm over his eyes. When he closed his eyes, he saw interesting colors. Damn good tea.

"What?"

"The thing with the car, the accident, the murder—it's all on tape, it went to the video store, someone took it out, I don't know where it is now...."

Omer leaned forward. Could a tape of the incident really be floating around after ten years? Could the tape have enough detail to recognize Sid by the light of the fiery wreck?

"This tape. Is Mr. Bifulco in it?"

"Yes, yes..."

"At the scene, where the murder of your...?"

"In the headlights. I can see it all. Can you imagine how this makes me feel, the thought of it on tape? Is there any more tea?"

"Where was the camera?"

"It was on the car seat, then on the ground." Russ waved one hand at the ceiling in a hopeless gesture. "It was on by accident—found it later—nobody knew. Can you buy this tea anywhere around here?"

"Not even the police?"

Russ yanked his arm from his eyes.

"Do you think I'd be here now if the police had the tape? I should have gone to the law in the first place. But I...hell, I was scared, I was..."

"Where is the tape now?" Omer was standing, finger raised thoughtfully to his lip. So Russ had evidence of his wife's murder all the while, but he was frightened for his own life should he go to the police.

"It was at the Show Time Videomat, Frustrumburg Shopping Center. In a box for *The Elvis Conspiracy.*"

Omer was momentarily transported back to Memphis, 1977, a late-night go-go bar, and a transaction with Presley's pharmacist.

"But somebody else took it out—somebody named Price." Russ sat up in agitation. "I'll heat some more water."

"What?" Omer spun around. The name on the bowling shirt, the cop at Chik's.

"Price," Russ repeated. "You want a cup?"

"Go ahead, take the thing."

"Me? That?" Price jumped to his feet.

"Well, you don't expect me to take it in for the reward? I'm on parole. I can't be hitched up to no rackets. Besides, you gotta earn your part of that reward, pal. Stuffing the fish is small beans. I'm the one that bagged it, after all!" Sid may have been in a tight spot, but he'd be damned if it kept him from driving a hard bargain.

Price wiped his hands nervously on his windbreaker and eyed the giant, white, tape-bound cooler.

"I dunno. What'll I say? I mean..."

"Tell 'em anything you want, pal. Tell 'em you found it in the trunk of your granny's Edsel. But if you want the five grand, you gotta earn it." Sid stood, grabbed Price by the sleeve, and led him to the cooler. Groaning, he hefted it into Price's arms. A grimace rippled over Price's face as the cooler pressed against the wound on his chest.

"There you go." Sid opened the door and began guiding Price outside. "But remember: it better be a good stuffing, and I want my five grand. Sure, I'm outta the rackets, and some guys might say I ain't got no teeth. But I got teeth. And I still bite, know what I mean? Be a good boy, now. Don't doublecross Bifulco." The guest was ushered reluctantly onto the porch.

"But what about the evidence? I've got..."

"Yeah? Certain parties find out about this deal an' I'll tell 'em how this was all your scam. You're the one wanted to play ball here, pal. So play. Beat it." Sid slammed the door and killed the porch light to drive his point home.

Price staggered into the dark driveway clutching the enormously heavy, creaky cooler. Aside from the throbbing pain of the bullet wound on his chest, all he could think about was the numbered pieces inside. This wasn't what he'd had in mind.

He supposed he could say he'd found it, but the Edsel bit was out.

chapter  17

Debbie got home and found her convalescent husband AWOL. It didn't surprise her. Price just better not be with that woman with the big tits. That bullet wound might reopen from those bazooms pounding against his chest.

Sure, Debbie knew, and it wasn't from any bras lying around the car. The bowling alley was a tempest of gossip. That's why she made her rendezvous with Chik in private. O.K., so she was pregnant. Should that stop her from doin' the dirty? Besides, Chik said it was kinky, and it did look hot on tape. All that red hair, her freckled belly like a honeydew melon, and on all fours barking like a dog.

Price would never go for doing videos, Debbie's secret habit from before marriage.

Why had she married Price? Hey, she wanted

kids, she didn't want to work, he had a good job and was well hung. He worked a number of nights, which allowed her to pursue her hobby. What more could a wife ask for?

So when she got home and Price wasn't there, Debbie wasted no time in giving in to her naughty tingling sensation.

At the VCR, she grabbed the rented French movie and found the empty *Elvis Conspiracy* box atop the VCR. Debbie noticed the VCR was still on and figured that Price had watched *The Elvis Conspiracy*. Popping the cassette from the VCR, she put it back in the *Elvis* box without registering its blank SUPER*PROCAM label. Tossing a third, blank TDK tape into her bag, she made for the car. Her plan was to run over to the Five Star and copy her latest "Chik Flick" onto the blank TDK tape. Her excuse for going back out if she should happen to run into Price?

To drop the rented tapes back at the Videomat.

It was the second time that evening that Bill the security guard found himself at the back door of the Show Time Videomat, only on this occasion he'd gotten called outta the can to respond. Bill was not happy about that. Neither were his bowels.

"Cockroaches! Cockroaches is what it is," Bill spat, sweat beading on the neck flesh rolled over his collar. He shone his light on the doorknob and along the jamb. No crowbar divots, no hammer marks.

Omer decided to forego stealth for expediency. He jabbed his umbrella into Bill's bacon. Mr. Phillips summoned a venomous tenor.

"Freeze! Don't move! I don't want to kill you, but I will if you turn around. Here. Cover your mouth with this. Hold it there and breathe deeply. Do it or I'll blow you to little bits!" And as Bill stood there with what he supposed was a gun in his love handle, drawing ether into his lungs from a hanky, he suddenly realized he was scared shitless. Literally.

He rolled onto the ground.

Some minutes later, as Omer scrolled down the computer screen, headlights splashed the front of the store. Motoring up to the facade of the Videomat, a car came to a sudden halt.

Omer's eyes narrowed, his jaw set, and his ears got pointier. Police? How? Why?

A silhouette cut through the headlights and stepped up to the glass door. Omer backed toward the rear exit. The front grates were still down and locked, so he'd have a few moments to slip away.

Bending over and turning sideways, the silhouette betrayed long hair and the ungainly crouching profile of a woman with a belly. There was a loud clatter.

"Shit!" the woman shouted. Omer could see her hurriedly picking tapes and tape boxes off the sidewalk, and then saw the return slot in the door flash.

A clatter of plastic sounded as two tapes entered the return bin and the pregnant silhouette headed back for the car.

Omer sighed. Of course. Only someone returning a tape into the after-hours slot. But the fleeting urgency put added flame under Omer's kettle. He set upon the computer screen again, whispering:

"Price, Price, Price..."

Not finding the tape marked as returned on the computer, he wondered if it had been dropped off after hours in the return bin. Lo and behold! Right on top of a bunch of DVD boxes was the shape of two VHS boxes. One was some French romance, the other *The Elvis Conspiracy*.

Smiling at his own cleverness, he popped open the case for *The Elvis Conspiracy* and fed the tape into a video player behind the counter.

Video snow.

Fast forward.

More snow.

He went all the way to the end of the tape.

Snow.

Omer frowned. The tape was blank, and so was the TDK label. He remembered the woman in silhouette who dropped her tapes and cursed, the sound of her putting the tapes back in the boxes. Was it possible that in the dark she put the blank tape in *The Elvis Conspiracy* box by accident?

Hope against hope, he opened the other VHS box; it contained the French romance tape. No luck.

That would mean Price—or his wife—still had the tape of Fest's killing.

chapter
18

The last thing Russ remembered was lying on the couch, talking to Phillips when...

Russ couldn't remember. He didn't remember Phillips leaving. He didn't even remember falling asleep.

Staggering into the bathroom, Russ splashed some rusty water on his face and looked in the mirror. It suddenly hit him. Russ had made a second cup of tea, sat back down, and Phillips pulled a penknife from his vest. He asked Russ whether he'd ever seen one like it.

Russ stared at the water dripping off his face and could hear Phillips saying: "You see, it's a very silver penknife, and it shines in the light, doesn't it, Russell? It sparkles, and isn't it soothing..."

"Damn! Hypnotized..." Russ said into the mirror, then drifted off to the living room where a quick accounting of his meager belongings revealed that nothing was taken, nothing was rifled. He found his teacup washed and in the drain board. Had he been drugged too?

Russ gripped his temples and stood in the center of his small musty living room, blood rushing through his brain, eyes tweaked tight. His mind was utterly aswirl with emotional clutter. Murder, videotapes, Sid, and a strange hypnotist.

Who were these people? How had this happened? Was it really happening? What was really happening?

Russ tried to picture his life only days before, when his biggest worry had been where the next sport was coming from or whether his truck would start or what magazine would dump the next rejection letter on him. Trivial stuff. If only he could trade today's devastated crop of problems for yesterday's spotty harvest of good news.

Something had to be done. Russ was a sitting duck for more evil twists of fate. If he sat at home, more doom would come knocking. He had to head it off. The fiasco must end.

Advice, he needed sage advice from someone outside the vexing circumstances. Someone to stick a pin in his bed, put his feet on the floor of reason, feed him the coffee of good sense, and get him awake, out of the nightmare. Phennel Rowe? No—

she'd just talk about embracing the Lord or something. She was a good listener, but Russ needed someone with his or her own feet on solid ground. O.K.—so he'd get in his truck—damn, in the shop. Wait, there was the Dodge. Hell, it hadn't been started in months. But Lloyd said . . . of course! Lloyd! A fellow motor-head—a man of reason. He'd probably be down at The Pond trying to talk someone into having their eyebrows done!

Racing about the room, he finally found the keys to the Dodge at the bottom of a mason jar full of rubber leeches.

Sure, the sign on the Five Star door said "CLOSED," but Chik's Camaro and a Jeep Cherokee said differently. Penelope was wise to Chik's ways. The dude was in there with another lady, "doin' tape." Many were the times that Penelope had been down in the "playroom" when a knock at the front door was ignored. Touché. She ran a hand over the doorsill and came up with the key. Holding it aimed at the lock, she paused and said, "Shit." What good would it do to barge in on their thing? She tucked the key back over the door.

She snapped a resentful bubble, folded her arms, and turned from the diner. Hey, she and Chik weren't exactly boyfriend and girlfriend, after all. She knew he did the dirty with other legs. Penelope did other guys, sometimes, when she could find one who wasn't freaked by the blinking red light of her camcorder. Unfortunately she didn't have one of those two-way mirrors like Chik had in the playroom.

Hopping her butt up onto the Camaro's hood, Penelope sighed and looked both ways on 241. Empty, and she had hitched to the Five Star. A single flood lamp high on a telephone pole pooled light in the dirt lot. She snapped a defiant bubble, bursting fog into the spring chill. The dark silhouette of Little Hound Mountain loomed in the darkness behind her and the diner. Moon was peeking over the trees to the east.

What really fried her fish was that she and Chik had, like, an appointment to "shoot some scenes," and damned if she didn't feel just an eensy bit jilted, stood up, taken for granted. Not jealous, no way.

Both hands found their way into her satiny chocolate hair and gave it some strategic tossing. Well, the night was young, she was ready for "tape," but she was short a dancing partner. If she could just hitch down the road to The Pond she might find someone there she knew, or didn't, as the case may be.

And just as she was thinking how the night seemed ripe for finally bagging Russ Smonig, she heard what sounded like a flimsy steam engine coming around the bend.

It all fit together. Lloyd, the man who knew motors inside and out, was the objective observer Russ needed to mediate his internal conflict. Methodical, logical, exacting, and mechanical-minded Lloyd, the straw at which Russ groped, was becoming a veritable Hercules of wisdom. As if hit by a bolt from Zeus, the Dodge had started, just like Lloyd said it would. O.K., so the engine was running on five out of six cylinders—well, maybe four—but it started. See, Lloyd was right!

Rounding the bend just shy of the Five Star, Russ punched the accelerator to see if he could burn the oil from the two fouled plugs and get all six rods rocking.

As the diner's sphere of light drew near, he could see someone waving her arms, walking to the road, jumping up and down.

Russ's foot came off the accelerator. It was Penelope.

Russ's foot went on the brake.

Sid answered the knock at the door expecting the taxidermist's return. Even though he'd foisted the fish on him, he knew the taxidermist wasn't entirely happy with the arrangement. So it took Sid a moment to realize who it was standing on his portico.

"Warden Lachfurst."

"By God, Bifulco, you're a free man! The name's Hillary Lachfurst. You can just call me Mr. Lachfurst."

The loud little man with the round specs pushed past Sid into the cabin, stopping at the center of the living room to take in his surroundings with the manner of Hannibal surveying the Alps. Finally, his eyes came to rest on Bifulco, who stood gripping a tumbler of Canadian, eyebrows seesaw-ing between confusion and astonishment.

"Uh, good to see you. Have to admit, I'm also a little *surprised* to see you." Sid took a halting step forward.

"What's that you're drinking?" Mr. Lachfurst waved one hand at Sid's tumbler and used the other to punctuate the remark with a slap to his hip boot.

"Canadian. You want some?"

"Don't happen to have any single malt?" Lachfurst tucked his thumbs into his fishing vest.

Sid drifted to the bar cart. He hadn't gotten around to stocking it for visitors.

"Nope. You, uh, want ice, Mr. Lachfurst?" Sid picked up a glass.

"You bet, and a little branch water if you please." Hannibal took to admiring the Alps again as Sid made for the kitchen and snapped an ice tray. When he returned, Mr. Lachfurst had one of Sid's fly rods in hand. He took the drink from Sid.

"Skoal." Lachfurst sipped, waggled the fly rod pensively, then turned on Sid. "I was at the Annual Correctional Administration Seminar in Scranton. Managed to spend part of the afternoon fishing Cherry Creek for brookies with a pal of mine who's a warden up at Erie. It was one of them days—pretty as all get-out—but the fish were down like nobody's business. It's happened before, of course. But there's a pattern at work here, Bifulco. Know what it is?"

"A pattern, Mr. Lachfurst?"

"Yep"—Lachfurst sipped, nodding all the while—"a pattern. What time of the month is it, Bifulco?"

The phrase "time of the month" had only one meaning for Sid, and it had to do with female bodily functions that interfered with male bodily functions.

"I'll tell you what time of the month it is, Bifulco. Two words: Full Moon. And do you know what that means?"

Werewolves?

"I'll tell you what that means. The fish feed at night, sleep during the day. So, why am I here, Bifulco?" Lachfurst slugged back a mouthful and fairly broke the glass putting it down.

"You wanna go fishing? Tonight?" Sid slugged back his drink and dropped the glass on the bar trolley. "Now?"

Mr. Lachfurst stepped up and gripped Sid's shoulder in a painful pinch. Light flashed off his specs. Sid didn't remember ever really seeing Warden Lachfurst's eyes.

"What did I always say, Sidney, out there on the athletic field?"

Sid puzzled a moment.

"You said, 'Initiative takes the day.'" Sid had never really understood what that meant.

"Well, Bifulco, I'm ready. Let us take the initiative. Let us take the fight to the fish. I'll go put my rod together, you put your boots on."

Mr. Lachfurst stiff-armed the screen door on the way to his Lexus.

Penelope, in her usual fashion, sat on a stool with her back against the bar. Elbows perched on the bar's edge, she arched her back in a way that only glorified her chest. Swiveling back and forth on her bar stool, she was making her way through a draft Yuengling, long sassafras hair draped across her face and cleavage, giving Russ sideways glances.

"So, Russ, the gang had a fine old time here last night, didn't we? 'Light me, Louie!'"

"What? Oh yeah, the, uh, thing..." Russ was half watching the bar's front door, half not watching Penelope's swiveling charms.

"Expecting someone?"

"What?"

"You seem distracted." Penelope rolled her head back and considered the glowing ducks on the wagon wheel overhead.

"Yeah, well, I gotta talk to Lloyd."

The Duck Pond was loosely packed, it being a Sunday night and all. It was just Russ, Penelope, and a group of four in bowling shirts eating microwave pizza.

"Can I ask you a question, Russ? Do you think Lloyd wants to hump me or what?"

A sip of beer almost came out of Russ's nose.

"Lloyd? What kind of question is that? He and Kris have lived together for..."

"So? I don't suppose he ever tol' you about the time he removed some pubies from my thighs?"

Russ's hands wrestled each other. This was a conversation he didn't want to have, not then.

"Well, Russ, it's not like anything happened or anything. Just the same, you can be sure he never tol' Kris about it. Never did get a bill. So, Russ, answer the question. Do you think Lloyd wants..."

"What kind of question is that? I can't... maybe I'll try him on the phone again." Russ poked his fedora brim up.

"You left two messages on his machine already."

Russ finished his beer, and the bartender gave them both a refill. Penelope began to swivel faster on her stool.

"What's eating you, Russ? Haven't you been getting your Wheaties?"

"Look, Penelope, I've got problems, O.K.? I gotta talk to Lloyd and..." Russ trailed off.

"You need to relax. You're all tied up in knots. Tell me what's bugging you. Maybe I can help get the kinks out." Penelope did a 360-degree spin on her stool.

"It's a wonder you don't already know..." Russ murmured.

"Maybe I already do."

"Ha! Boy...wouldn't that take the cake." Russ

just shook his head at the thought, turning to the sound of a bowler exiting.

"Ever look at dirty magazines?"

"Jesus, Penelope!"

"I do. I think they're hot. What about videos?"

"Please, Penelope..." Russ put his hand over his eyes.

"I think videos are hot."

"I've had quite enough of videos today," Russ said through clenched teeth.

"What, *Bass Almanac* videos? Or were you makin' one of your own?"

"Never mind."

"Were you in a video? Huh?"

Russ blanched and looked at her through his fingers.

"Is that what it was?"

Russ took his hand from his face and put it on his beer, taking a sizable gulp.

"See, maybe I know all about it, like you said. A tape, just you and a friend or two up to a little no-good at night, am I right?"

Russ avoided her eyes.

"Out there in the woods, out there in the dirt and gravel."

He fixed a twitching eye at her.

"Did Jenny tell you? Damn, Sid said he didn't..."

"Jenny, huh? Maybe. Maybe a little bird told me."

Forehead to the bar, Russ moaned: "Is there

anybody who doesn't know about my problems? Anybody?"

When Debbie walked in the door, she was relieved to find that Price still wasn't home. She figured he must have gone over to Ted's Tap Room for a beer. Her intent had been to rush back home, but Chik had something in the playroom to show her, and next thing she knew she was wearing a ten-gallon hat, chaps, and her birthday suit. Then she was lassoing Chik, who galloped about the playroom in Holstein-spotted leotards. And all in front of that two-way mirror.

Well, it was a quickie, sort of a dry run, so to speak, of a larger movie idea. And it had taken longer than Debbie had realized. Chik handed her the tape of the evening's romp. As she headed to the door, he asked her whether she'd brought a blank tape.

"In the plastic bag on the counter—gotta run," she said.

Huffing and puffing up the stairs from the Five Star's basement, she lugged her unborn porn star to her Jeep Cherokee and sped home.

As soon as she was home and realized Price was out, Debbie just had to pop in the new dirty video for a quick look. The evening's exertion weighed heavily upon her as she picked up the remote and prepared to sit in Price's chair.

That's when her water broke and she realized the baby was on the way. She hobbled to the neighbors, who rushed her down to Methodist Hospital, from where they tried unsuccessfully to reach Price by phone.

Lunar shine flowed over the riverbank, setting the chop and riffles alight in platinum flash. Oars gouged the onyx river, the splashes tossing opaline sparks toward the full moon. Lachfurst was rowing, and his specs shimmered in Sid's direction.

"Well, I'm driving. Where you been takin' them?"

"Mr. Lachfurst, I've only been here three days."

"Tonight is a night for taking the bastards on the surface. I'll tell you what: We'll do the inside shore, right where the shallows drop off. What do you say? Good!" The fast current had just swung the boat downstream when Mr. Lachfurst spat on his palms and set upon the oars with gusto. With an even, steady stroke, Lachfurst crossed the channel with speed and few bumps. For all his squawking, Sid mused, this bird Lachfurst seemed to know how to flap those wings. In short order the boat drifted under the shadow of the trees on the far bank, and Lachfurst hopped out of the boat.

"Come on, Bifulco. Let's go find a good spot." Standing in the shallows, Lachfurst pulled the bow onto shore. "It's time you got your butt outta that boat and stood like a man in this noble river."

There was a flash of spectacles, then the crunch of the Warden's boots through the forest.

Battling vines and roots in the night, Sid caught up with Mr. Lachfurst some minutes later in a moonlit clearing where a huge tree felled by floodwaters had swept the vegetation to one side. Mr. Lachfurst plowed into the rocky river up to his knees before he stopped, tucked his rod under one arm, and pulled out a fly box.

"Now here's a dandy spot. Come on out here, Bifulco. I got a fly for yah that'll drive 'em nuts!"

Still panting from his tussle with the dark thicket, Sid waded out to Mr. Lachfurst. What had he done to deserve a visit from Lachfurst? He hadn't even bagged the girl in the red hikers, hadn't actually evoked the curse.

"Here. Know what fly that is?" The specs flashed moonlight in Sid's eyes.

"Yeah, sure, it's a really big black Wulff." Sid looked around to see if anybody else was crazy enough to be out there—perhaps even goons from the local anglers' syndicate.

"A black fly cuts a starker contrast against the moonlit sky, makes a darker shadow. Here, tie that on. I've got another one in here—there it is."

Lachfurst handed him the other fly, and Sid eyed it skeptically. Most trout flies were delicate little things designed to tempt the dainty appetite of fussy fish. If those were profiteroles, this was a porterhouse steak with all the trimmings.

Once they'd tied on, Mr. Lachfurst began the demonstration, but not before grabbing Sid's shoulder again.

"You ready, Bifulco? Good. Look downstream. What do you see?"

Riffles.

"I'll tell you what I see. A fish rising, just below a rock."

Mr. Lachfurst pulled his line out and false cast. Squinting at the flinty riffles, Sid saw no fish rising, no fins or tails, and he doubted whether Mr. Lachfurst did either, other than in his imagination. The night was too dark, the fly was too dark, and no trout in his right mind would go for a giant black fly. He gave Mr. Lachfurst credit for being a guy with good tackle, and a guy who knew how to cast and row, but he always sort of figured Lachfurst was an armchair angler, one who liked his tales tall as his drinks.

About fifteen minutes passed, during which each of Mr. Lachfurst's casts was followed by an excuse like "bad drift," "wrong mend," "fly landed sideways," or "cursed foolish bastard, doesn't know a meal ticket when he sees one!"

And just as Sid was beginning to arch his back and shuffle his feet, line ripped the current and spray filled the air.

"Ha!" Lachfurst nudged Bifulco with his elbow as he stripped in the fly line. A burst of glittering spray spat a pirouetting trout into the air. It landed with a slap and raced upstream in the heavy current.

"Holy Mother of God! Was that the one you been casting to?"

"Nope. This is the other one." Lachfurst plowed a few steps upriver, following the fish with his rod tip.

"There was more than one?"

"Sid, there are a whole bunch of fish in this river. Soon as I land this monster, we'll get you one. Now watch. Are you watching, Bifulco? This is how we land a fish. See, lead him into the shallow water directly upstream, get a rod's length of line between rod tip and fish, net in one hand, rod in other, you bring him down, let him face upstream, put the net behind to one side, then turn him quickly—oops, wait a minute…here…he…comes…aaand scoop!"

Lachfurst lunged, missed, lunged again, and lofted the drenched wriggling net. He growled contentedly and turned back to his pupil, net extended. Sid looked down at a sixteen-inch rainbow trout twisting like a tube of quicksilver in the moonlight, big black Wulff in one corner of its mouth. The trout's flat chrome pupil tilted at Lachfurst. Sid wondered if the fish could actually see them, actually know what he'd just gotten himself into, whether he blamed the fly or himself for getting him in dutch.

A second later, Lachfurst was dipping the net back in the water, and in a mercurial flash the trout was gone.

* * *

Price screeched his truck to a halt in the driveway. In his haste to get to the den, he not only failed to see the note stuck to his front door but also the Karmann Ghia that rolled to a stop across the street.

By the time Omer got to peeking through the yew hedge and into the living room window, Price had a videotape in one hand, a phone receiver in the other. Next to him on an end table Omer noticed a photo of Price and redhead Debbie on their wedding day. Price had his jacket on, and Omer could read lips well enough to see him say "I'll come over right now. I've got something big to show you."

There was no time to waste. Mr. Phillips marched himself over to the front of Price's pickup, put his umbrella tip through the grille, and turned the crook. A sharp metallic note sounded as a small spring-loaded spike punctured the radiator.

"Penelope, what the hell are we doing here? The Five Star doesn't open for another six hours."

She tossed him an impish smile, left the car, and walked across the pool of light to the diner.

Russ killed the Dodge's rattling engine and followed reluctantly. There were no cars in the lot. A few crazed moths lusted over the flood lamp above.

Penelope retrieved the key from over the door.

"Penelope, I don't think we ought to—where'd you get that key? You know, I don't think Chik would appreciate..."

Penelope pulled him into the diner by his sleeve and swung the door shut.

"What is this, Penelope? What are we doing here?"

She sashayed behind the counter and paused next to the potted palms.

"You want that tape, don't you? Well..."

She led him downstairs. Confusion was Russ's first reaction to Chik's basement playroom. He didn't get it. What were all the mirrors for, and the lights? On one wall was a Peg-Board loaded with chains, whips, silk scarves, strips of leather, and rope. Half the floor was done over in wrestling mats, a Jacuzzi gurgled against the far wall, and a sawhorse was piled high in fake leopard, zebra, tiger, and polar bear skins. Penelope flicked a series of switches—a phony fireplace crackled and a rack system played a CD of Zulu war chants. She disappeared around the corner as drums thrummed to soaring tribal choruses.

"What in God's name is this? It's like a, uh, rec room or something. I didn't know Chik had this. He could put a pool table down here." Russ unzipped his jacket and slid his hat back. "Boy, he keeps it warm in here, doesn't he? So where's the tape, Penelope?" Russ wandered over to a small wet bar, the top of which was littered with videotapes and boxes.

His eyes stung when he saw it, and an exclamation caught in his throat. Russ pounced on *The Elvis Conspiracy*. Trembling fingers snapped it open. The SUPER*PROCAM label was blank. But it just had to be the one.

"Yes! Yes!" Russ held the SUPER*PROCAM tape high and bounced on his toes, a Zulu warrior in high spirits. He whipped around when he heard Penelope reenter.

"Yes?" she purred, stirringly shrink-wrapped in a black rubber bikini.

"OO!" the Zulus shouted, stopped, then drummed spears on their shields.

Russell Smonig had been on a twenty-four-hour emotional roller coaster, from one extreme to the next. But Penelope really threw him for a loop.

They say every man has his breaking point. But when it comes to sex, most bend instead.

Price's pickup was barreling up Route 52 toward Frustrumburg when a red light on the dash interrupted the latest of his practiced speeches.

"Captain, I had to come right over tonight because the man who shot me is in this cooler, and I have the videotape. Aw, dang!" Price pounded the steering wheel with a fist as he saw the overheat light.

He pulled over onto the narrow dirt shoulder of the lonely road in the middle of the night. There was no denying that his isolation scared him just a little bit, but he shrugged it off best he could, blew into his hands, and opened the hood. A great billow of steam vomited forth. He reiterated, "Aw, dang!"

Price flapped his arms helplessly at his side. There was nothing he could do, much less see, until the engine cooled off, so he shoved his mitts in his windbreaker and paced in the beams of his headlights.

O.K., so he'd give that guy Bifulco half the reward. Well, $5,000 anyway. That is, the reward was actually a hundred thousand smackeroos, and damned if Price didn't intend on making most of that his. "After all, it was *me* that got shot, it is *me* who deserves monetary compensation." Price nodded in agreement with himself.

That was ninety-five thousand bucks he had coming, which was enough to pay off the mortgage on his house and buy a bass boat, one of those slick-looking ones they had in the catalogs, home delivered. Would a U.S. Post Office truck trailer it to his front door or what? Hell, it sure as shit wouldn't come in a box.

The mortgage? Did he really feel like blowing all that moolah on the bank? Sure, there were all sorts of things he'd *like* to spend the bucks on, like debauched vacations in the Caribbean or New Orleans. He'd never forgotten the Brotherhood of Troopers convention two years ago in Atlantic City. But he had a wife, and a kid on the way, and responsibility. Maybe he'd pay off a big chunk of the mortgage, get the boat, and put a slice of the pie aside in a "Motel Fund." He liked the sound of that. It sounded sneaky: "Motel Fund."

The growl and sputter of a sports car shifting gears wafted up the road, and Price got ready to wave the passerby down. It would probably be someone he knew. And it was—sort of.

Omer squeaked his car to a stop, engine a-sputter. He lapsed into his Five Star Diner persona.

"Well, friend, looks like you got a little car trouble. Radiator, is it? You know, that reminds me of Tommy Peason—you know him? He once lost all his transmission fluid, just like that, and—"

"You headed to Frustrumburg?" Price interrupted.

"Well, as a matter of fact, I am going that way. I was just heading home. Live up by Quinn's place. Know it? It's that gray house with the porch and the yellow Lab. I think the dog's name is Ryan. Or is it Bristol?"

"Look, could you give me a ride—just about two miles up the road? You probably know the place. It's in that development—Boxwood."

"Boxwood? Sure I know it. There's a cousin of mine who lives in St. Louis who has a bungalow on the Missouri River on Candlewood Drive. Not Boxwood, of course, but it always reminds me when I pass the sign. That is, the sign for Boxwood always—"

"Great! Thanks a lot, lemme get my stuff."

A moment later Omer was helping Price strap the cooler to the luggage rack. As Price leaned over, the videotape fell from the inside pocket of his windbreaker onto the floor of the car.

"Dang."

"I got it..." Omer saw his opportunity and stabbed a hand into the dark recess.

"No, let me..."

"Here." Omer handed him the tape and Price quickly stuffed it back into his jacket.

chapter  **20**

Eggs sizzled on the grill next to a pile of greasy home fries. Steam jetted steadily from the coffee silo. Buckwheats and a side of honeydew completed the breakfast special. Morning had arrived along with rain clouds, and the usual crew appeared at Chik's.

The Bobs stood solemnly in ponchos at the counter awaiting their order. The English muffins were taking their own sweet time toasting. Jenny, decked out in a yellow rainsuit, squeezed in the front door behind them.

"Good mornin', fellahs. Hey, Little Bob, where's that camera of yours? I thought that thing was surgically attached to your hand."

The Bobs avoided her eye, but she persisted.

Jenny nudged Big Bob in the waist and looked up at him.

"Rent any good tapes lately, boys?" Jenny winked and headed down the counter to her seat at the end. The Bobs didn't say a word. They blushed instead.

"Here's cup number one, Jenny." Chik slid a cup of coffee in front of her. "Say, today's your day off, babe. What're ya doing up this early? Thought you might catch me alone, get me to slip you the wood?" Chik flashed her his sauciest smile.

Jenny's quickly raised hand made Chik duck for cover.

"Don't ya call me 'babe,' weasel face. Next time I'll smack ya."

Chik snickered and put a pencil tick on the side of the coffee urn.

Lloyd entered with furrowed brow, shaking rain off his jean jacket, and when he saw the Bobs, he sidled up next to them. He whispered: "Ya guys see Russ recently?"

They shrugged.

"I got some real strange—hell, I'd say desperate—calls on my machine last night. Tell ya the truth, I'm a little worried. Tried calling him at home. On and off, all night. No answer. His messages said he called from the Duck Pond, but by the time I rang there they was closed. Think we oughta head over to his place?"

The Bobs looked from Lloyd to each other.

"Darn it, he's suicidal, I tell ya," Big Bob muttered. "Never second-guess *Newstime*."

Meanwhile, Chik served Jenny two eggs Jersey-side, whisky down.

"So what's got ya up so early on your day off, Jenny?"

"Got a lead on a good shad spot. Figured a nice drizzly day might be the best time to take advantage of it." She stabbed the eggs with the toast and they bled yolk.

"Uh-huh—another secret shad spot, I'll bet." Chik twisted his dishrag. "Ya fishing from shore?"

"Cool your jets. That guy Bifulco owes me a favor. He's showing me the spot, so I don't know where it is yet. But I got my boat out there on the trailer. Gonna launch it at the Mink Run boat ramp, motor up to his place."

The front door slammed shut and the toaster popped simultaneously. Chik pivoted and froze.

"Hey, where'd the Bobs go? Their muffins is done."

Sid had only been asleep for three hours when a pounding on his door jarred him awake.

"Sid!" Russ was shouting. "Sid! Wake up! Sid, I've got the tape!"

Still in his plaid shirt and pants from the night before, Bifulco wobbled to his feet from the couch and fell upon the doorknob.

"Would you keep it down, for Christ sake!" he rasped. "You wanna wake Lachfurst or what? Jeez!"

Even in his sleep-deprived state, Sid noticed something different about Russ. Granted, the goofy smile and sparkly eye were different, and Sid supposed he hadn't seen Russ with his collar up or his fedora full of rainwater before. But it wasn't any of that, or the videotape in one hand. Sid looked him top to bottom. Russ's grin twitched.

"Sid, I got the tape! Look! In my hand!"

Bifulco's eye slipped past Russ to the Dodge in the drive. He could see Penelope asleep in the passenger seat.

"Russ, your shoes are on backward," Sid noted. "You get lucky last night or what?"

Tripping over the stoop, Russ pushed past Sid.

"Where's your TV?" He flashed annoyance, then disappointment at his misfit sneakers.

Sid gently pulled the door shut.

"Hey, Captain Fedora, you wanna keep it down? Like I said, we don't wanna wake Lachfurst."

Russ sat on the edge of the couch and pried off one sneaker, then the next.

"Look, Sid, all we gotta do is take a peek at the tape, make sure it's the right one, then rip it to shreds!"

"Yo, Smonig, there's a warden from a federal penitentiary in the next room." Sid wagged a finger in front of Russ's nose. "I don't think we want him to see it."

"A what?" Russ started putting his left sneaker on his right foot again.

"A warden from a federal penitentiary. An old

friend, so to speak. Showed up last night. And the TV is in there, in my bedroom, right where he's sleeping. So where'd you get the tape?"

"What difference does that make?" Russ reddened. "Sid, the sooner we make sure this is the tape, the sooner I can destroy it and go back to life's simpler pleasures, like slowly going broke and being depressed." Russ blurted, "I don't have a video setup. You do."

Forget that Sid had only three hours' Z's in his hat. After an enterprising career as hood, murderer, rat, and felon, it took a lot to fluster him. Frankly, he didn't see the big deal. The tape was recovered. Hooray. So Russ holds on to it very tightly for a couple hours, a couple days, whatever. As far as Sid was concerned, the video crisis was over. Russ was being a schmoe.

"Would you keep it down! Look, I'll go in there and get the equipment, give it to you, you take it over to your little shack and watch the tape. But you gotta promise something: stay away from me, 'cause I don't want any part of whatever rackets you're into. Deal?"

Russ fitted the right shoe on his left foot.

"Hold it, hold it. I thought the deal was that I was beholden to you for, you know, and that I had to show you the river. Now you're saying you don't want free guiding? You release me from that obligation?"

"That's right. That's right. I don't want any part of your rackets."

"Rackets?"

"Would you keep it down?"

"All right, all right—what the hell do you mean 'rackets'?"

There was a knock at the door.

"Must be your girlfriend got tired of waitin'."

They both pulled the door open a crack.

"Frank," Russ burbled, "what brings you here?"

"Frank who?" Sid quizzed aloud.

"T-taxidermist," Frank stuttered from under a handlebar mustache.

"Sorry, I already have a—wait, you're Frank Highly?"

"Taxidermist," Frank replied again. "I know I was s-s'posed to come last night, b-but it got real late an' I th-thought..."

Sid pulled the door all the way open, stepped out onto the porch, and locked a familial arm around Frank's long neck, turning him away from the cabin.

"You're the taxidermist I called, that right?"

Frank blinked and gave a nervous tug at his mustache.

"You b-betcha. And you're Sid, the guy that c-called me about a c-carp?"

"And you're the guy that said you'd come by last night and pick up the fish on your way back from Honesdale, am I right?"

Frank rolled his eyes at Sid, then let them spring back to fix on his red VW Bug.

"H-honesdale, you b-betcha."

"Don't you have a friend, an assistant, that you sent over last night to pick up the fish?" A smile played with the mole on Sid's cheek, as if he really expected to hear the answer he wanted.

Frank blinked and rolled his eyes over at Sid.

"N-n-" Frank didn't finish. He just shook his head.

"Should I even bother asking you—Frank—who it was then that came by and took my big fish?"

"N-n-" Frank blinked hard.

"O.K., Frank." Sid unclasped his chummy hold and forced a handshake on him. "I'll find out where the fish is, I'll get the fish back, and I'll get the fish to you. O.K.? Thanks for stopping by. I appreciate it, really. You're a prince." Sid shooed Frank toward his Bug, which the latter mechanically boarded.

Sid waved until Frank putt-putted out of sight. Then he turned on Russ.

"Some friggin' bastard stole my fish, and you're gonna tell me who it was." Sid pushed up on his T-shirt sleeves.

"Me? What the hell?" Russ tripped over the doorsill. "Who would steal your carp?"

"Some guy shows up last night, right about the time this taxidermist was supposed to show, and asks for the fish. Then he tells me there's a reward for the fish, and in fact says that I better hand over half the reward for him to stuff it. And do you know why? Because I caught the thing with you. You're out to fix this reward deal. You're some kinda guy on the inside of the local rackets and you tried to make the favorite lose or something. I dunno. I don't got it figured out yet, but frankly, Smonig, I don't wanna figure it out."

"Wait a minute, wait a minute, wait a minute. Do you mean to say you think I'm, like, involved in some kind of betting operation? On fish?"

It did sound a little far-fetched, suddenly, when Russ said it aloud.

"Look, Sid, if some guy showed up here last night with that yarn, well, all I can say is he must have been pulling your leg."

"A guy I don't even know comes by and pulls my leg for no reason? Hey, the guy said he knew all about the fish. He said he knew you and me whacked it and that there was a $10,000 reward."

Russ scratched his forehead. "And you're sure he was talking about a fish?"

"Of course I'm sure. In fact, I joked that I'd chopped it up into little pieces to fit it into... uh-oh."

"What? 'Uh-oh' what?"

"It's possible he was talkin' about that other thing."

"What other thing?"

Sid shot Russ an exasperated look. "Jimmy Spaghetti."

"But how? Who is he?"

"He musta seen the tape, maybe rented it outta the video store by accident. This guy knew about what happened with Jimmy and was tryin' to shake me down."

"And you gave him the carp." Russ lowered slowly until he was sitting on the portico steps. "We're done for."

"Like hell! You got the tape, right? That guy—if he doesn't have it, he's got no evidence. No corpus delicti. Assuming, of course, that's the tape."

They both stared at the tape in Russ's hands for a moment before Sid spoke again.

"I'll get my VCR. We'll take the tape over to your place."

chapter **21**

Like most hospitals, Methodist treated visitors like weasels seeking admission to a henhouse. First they confiscated his massive cooler. Then they tersely explained that each patient is allowed only two visitors, and that as the two neighbors who ferried Debbie to the hospital were still upstairs, Price wouldn't be allowed up to the ward. When he told them he was the expectant father, they told him to prove it. And so it was that Trooper Price, without a wallet, bolted past the desk and up the stairs, where he proceeded to get lost, then found—by the security guards. After a short tussle, they said they'd escort him to the maternity ward and have the mother or someone else there identify him. But the neighbors had left without returning their passes to the front desk, and the mother was in the process of giving birth. In a subsequent argument and another tussle, Price's windbreaker was torn open. His bowling shirt was exposed, along with his name embroidered on the breast pocket. Security supposed that would suffice.

As if his little visit to Captain Reuster hadn't been abusive enough. It was at the captain's house, after the presentation of the tape he had grabbed from his VCR and an iced carp, that Price had heard the news he was an imminent father. Reuster had driven him down to Methodist, tootling his kooky nasal laugh all the way. He'd chalked up Price's bizarre presentation of the fish to the frazzled nerves of an expectant father compounded by posttraumatic shock from his bullet wound. Condescendingly, Reuster had given the brooding, bloodshot Price another week off to recover.

Twins. Twin girls. Price had two daughters. Was he happy about it? He didn't know. Boys were what he wanted, of course. That and the reward of $95,000. With two kids he could use it more than ever.

Price hadn't smoked since he left the army, but he bought half a pack of generic cigarettes for two bucks from a passing custodian. He stepped out into the parking lot and started making his way through a couple as he paced. It seemed the thing to do.

That Bifulco was a sharp cookie, sticking him with that carp. But what about the video? It had to be that jackass from the Five Star Diner who drove the sports car. Did he pull a switch on Price? Was he part of Bifulco's gang?

Well, the point was, Price still knew what he knew about Sid, and that had to carry some weight. Damn straight. If he wanted to, he could make waves for a parolee like Bifulco, which is exactly what Sid wouldn't want. Shit, even an accusatory letter to the parole board could put a bird like that back in the cage. Price might even be able to sic the local law on it, even the FBI. There would be reason enough to think Fest had been headed for Bifulco, and with Sid's record, reason enough to expect that there might be a deadly confrontation. A close look at the truck and a little forensic work along the driveway might even turn up hard evidence.

Price stomped on his smoke and went back inside. He snuck a look in on Debbie. She was fast out, mouth partially open, a snore in the making, and gaunt like she'd just had the flu. Even still, that red hair and all those freckles warmed a spot in Price's heart. She was a good wife, he thought, and she'd doubtless be a better mother. How long would it be before they could fool around? Just like on their first anniversary, he reckoned they might bee-line for the Buck 'n' Doe on Route 32. For old time's sake. Price was particularly fond of that motel.

Collecting his hefty cooler from the leery admissions desk, Price proceeded to roust a sleeping taxi driver parked in the hospital driveway.

* * *

"You are, of course, the local pornography expert, aren't you?" Omer might as well have said Chik was the world's best chef.

Casting a sly and jaunty look around his domain, Chik warmed Omer with a grin. "You might say that."

Omer drew a little closer over the counter. "I'd even go so far as to guess that you're up on all the latest tapes too. Know all the stars, all their 'peculiarities.' Am I right?"

"You might say that." Chik twirled his spatula.

"Might you even know of a pregnant redheaded woman?"

Chik's gaze stuck to the end of his spatula. The toothpick in his teeth waggled uneasily beneath his mustache.

"You see, by accident, I got hold of a certain piece of cinema with this redheaded woman. Dressed up like a cowboy—in chaps and little else—she ropes a cow that turns out to be a bull, if you get what I mean."

"Say, what is this?" Chik felt some kind of shakedown coming on. "How'd you get hold of that tape?"

"I'll be quite frank with you, Mr. Chik. I'm working on a long shot here. I'm not making any trouble for you. In fact, here's fifty dollars for all the help you've been. Go on, take it, you've earned it."

Chik made the bill disappear.

In the corner booth, Phennel Rowe had finished her daily Ovaltine. She had her hip boots on, and there was a bucket and shovel in the backseat of her '59 Chrysler Imperial just outside. She waved a Gideon Bible at Chik as her way of signaling for the check. He processed her fifty cents and escorted her out to her car. The doors to the thing were heavy as casket lids, and Phennel had one hell of a time getting them open by herself. As Chik held the driver's door for her, she slipped a finger in his shirt pocket and pulled his face down to hers. Big wet eyes ogled his curious beady peepers.

"Mr. Chik, don't ask how I know, but there's somethin' fearful goin' on around here. Reverend Jim Chattanooga and I will pray for you."

Phennel lifted her fingers out of his pocket and promptly eased sidesaddle into her car. She swung her legs in and Chik closed the door. A customary wave good-bye was replaced by a poke in his direction with the Gideon Bible.

When Chik stepped back into the Five Star, he rang up Omer's fifty cents' worth of tea on the register. "You're not going to make any trouble? For her? For me?"

"Let's put it this way." Omer smiled. "If you don't tell me who she is, I will make trouble. I'll even make it easy for you. Is her name Price?"

Chik nodded, wide-eyed.

"Married to a trooper?"

Chik nodded again.

"And can I assume he doesn't know about this tape? Possibly others?"

"Damn, how do you know so much, Mr. Phillips?"

Omer reflected on the wedding photo from Price's living room. "Observation, Mr. Chik, close attention to detail."

Lachfurst stumbled from the bedroom and flung open the front door to Ballard Cabin.

"First it was a small squirrel slipping in the window and biting my nostril." Lachfurst growled like a bear fresh from his den. "Then it was people creeping into the room futzing with videotape equipment. Now it's some ingrate banging on the door. Jumpin' Jehovah's Fat! Can't a man get some shut-eye?"

"Where's Bifulco?" Price sneered, dropping the cooler on the porch.

"How the dickens should I know! Come back later!" Lachfurst no sooner slammed the door than Price started pounding again.

The door opened slowly. Warden Lachfurst tugged the sash of Sid's red satin bathrobe. He smoothed back his scalp and adjusted his specs. Shoving open the screen door, he stepped out onto the porch. He squared his stance, folded his arms, and flashed his specs up into Price's eyes. Lachfurst lowered his voice.

"What I think we have here, friend, is a bona fide misunderstanding. You want to talk to Mr. Bifulco, isn't that right?"

Price poked his chin defiantly at Lachfurst, but before he could say anything, the Warden continued.

"Then why, friend, do you keep trying to talk to me? I told you he wasn't here, didn't I? And yet you banged on that door again. I must assume, then, that you have something to say to me, is that right? Well, say your piece and then just get the hell out of here. Do we understand each other?"

"His car is right over there, so don't tell me he's not around here somewhere." Price squinted, clenching his jaw. "Now look, buster, I wanna know where Bifulco is, and I wanna know now, see? I'm not afraid of your type. I know how to deal with sleaze like you."

Lachfurst glanced at Sid's LTD and the girl in Russ's Dodge rubbing her eyes. He refolded his arms.

"Look, sonny, I don't know where Sid is, and I don't know where you come off with this 'sleaze' business. You don't know me from a sober Sunday! If that cooler's for Bifulco, just put it on the porch and get your silly ass offa this property—pronto."

"Bifulco can have his 'fish' back. Some joke." Price brandished a finger and poked Lachfurst in the solar plexus. "But Johnny Fest is no joke. Just tell him that. Just tell him Johnny Fest is going to come back to haunt him."

Lachfurst had heard about Fest's escape and, in fact, that was part of the reason he'd chosen to visit Sid when he did. All he really knew about Johnny's physical appearance, though, was that he was big, tough, and armed. He gave Price the once-over.

A huge pistol bulged at his waist. Initiative takes the day.

Lachfurst's left hook glanced off "Fest's" chin, but his right was blocked by Fest's left. The porch railing cracked and the two crashed into the daffodils, mulch and buttery petals flying with each chopping blow. The Warden punched at Fest's midsection. Price kicked and elbowed the "gangster." Hands under chins, fists in guts, arms around necks, the two rolled in the wet topsoil. Lachfurst grabbed for the gun, got hold of the barrel, and yanked it from the desperado's torn windbreaker.

Price grabbed the butt and snatched it back. Lachfurst pushed away, panting and muddy, and stood with his back up against the shingles of Ballard Cabin. Price's shaky hands targeted the barrel at the Warden's head.

Somewhere behind Lachfurst's specs, his pupils dilated in anticipation. Not anticipation of death or gunfire, but of what would happen when Penelope swung her shovel.

A resounding tympanic B-flat scrambled Price's gray matter. His world buzzed, twirling fuzzily about him, a reality composed of houseflies. It wasn't so much painful as paralyzing, loud, and indistinct. He didn't feel the mud that pushed into his face when he fell forward.

"Bully, my girl, bully!" Lachfurst snatched the .45 automatic from the ground. Wiping mud from his forearms and spitting more from his lips, he put the safety catch on the gun and popped out the clip.

Penelope stood with the shovel right where she had been when the flat of the spade had struck Price's head.

"Feh. Clip is empty! A tiger with no teeth!" Lachfurst snapped the clip back in place and tucked the .45 under the sash of his borrowed bathrobe.

"Who is he?" Penelope asked breathlessly.

"The man you just apprehended, my girl"—Lachfurst took the shovel from her hands and threw it aside—"is a desperate fugitive bent on murder: Johnny Fest. I am the honorable Warden Hillary Lachfurst, friend and mentor of the new, improved Sid Bifulco, squire and angler."

"Oh. Is he, like, dead? I never, y'know, hit anybody—like that—with a shovel."

"Let's find out." Lachfurst stretched out a foot and rolled Price over.

Blood stirred in Price's brain. He awoke suddenly, rolled away from Lachfurst, and snapped to wobbly legs. Mud blackened his face. Soil plopped off his arms. He blinked hard, gasping.

"O.K., fellah, it'll do you no good now, no good at all." Lachfurst pointed an instructional finger. Price backed slowly away.

"Better turn yourself in, Johnny. The police'll be here any minute. There's no use running off."

Price shook his noggin and put a hand to the back of his head. He winced savagely.

"You got a nasty bump there, Fest. Maybe a concussion. Your chest is bleeding too. Better get you to the prison hospital, patch you up...." Lachfurst took another step toward the fugitive.

"Prison? Hospital? F-Fest...I'm not, I'm not..."

"Whoever you are, you're going to prison, son. Now come on, let's get you in handcuffs or something...."

Price bolted, tripping and crashing into the woods.

Clearly exhausted, Lachfurst held his ground, a fatherly, outstretched hand still extended. But he let the hand drop and turned to Penelope.

"There are some people who just refuse help. I guess we'll have to call in the authorities to round him up."

"Hey," Penelope began, giving Lachfurst a foxy eye, "don't I know you? Aren't you the guy who stopped in at the Duck Pond last year in the fall?"

Lachfurst's eyebrows jumped and he adjusted his specs.

"Duck Pond?"

Penelope put one hand on her hip, the other held a finger out at Lachfurst.

"Yeah, and you'd just come from a meeting, an annual conference or something—of school principals, in Scranton."

"Hm, doesn't, uh, sound likely..." Lachfurst was suddenly busy brushing off his robe.

"Sure, and after a few drinks, you started telling me that as a principal of a girls' school, you had to, like, discipline the girls? Don't tell me you don't remember." Penelope folded her arms over her ample chest.

Lachfurst was confronted by her pouting grin and searching eye. He straightened his lapels, adjusted his specs, and gave Penelope the once-over, as if it were the first time he'd really taken a close look at her. He cleared his throat.

"Ah yes. Yes. I seem to remember that we discussed discipline."

Penelope's grin twisted wickedly, and Lachfurst brought a soiled satin arm around her shoulder, guiding her to the cabin.

"Yes, of course I remember, my child. And as I recall, you had been skipping class."

"Nice place you got here, Smonig," Sid said with what little sincerity he could muster. He was giving the place the once-over while Russ hooked up the VCR to his 13-inch black-and-white TV. Sid winced at the tiny kitchenette and warped, water-stained ceiling, strolled past a nicely mounted brown trout, and approached Russ's fly-tying bench. His eye latched onto a framed photo on the wall. Sid cleared his throat.

"Russ?"

"Yeah?" Russ was busy trying to plug the VCR into an already crowded extension cord.

"Who's this in the photo?"

Russ glanced up and paled slightly.

"That's me. And my wife."

"Your wife?"

"She's dead."

"No shit?"

"Car crash."

"Jeez, sorry to hear that." Sid turned away from the photo and stuck the SUPER*PROCAM tape in the VCR, calculating eyes avoiding Russ. "You used to have a beard?"

"Yeah." Russ pushed a button to rewind the tape. "That was a long time ago."

Sid eyed a hatchet that lay nearby on the kitchen counter.

"In Hartford?"

"Yes." Russ looked quizzically at Sid as he pushed the PLAY button. "Who told you that?"

Sid shrugged. "A lucky guess."

The TV was turned up loud, and Big Bob's voice blared from the speaker, "Holy bejesus, Russ!" followed by Little Bob saying "Oh boy, oh boy!"

Russ took a step toward Sid, and his voice trembled.

"You...you know something, don't you? It wasn't an accident, was it?"

Sid's dark eyes were on the hatchet. He had a couple of options at his disposal.

"You wanna know who killed her, is that it?"

The TV blared: "Watch it, Little Bob, Russ is gonna faint!" followed by "He's too heavy!" and a dull thud.

Russ's jaw tensed, but he said nothing.

"And you wanna know why, too, am I right?" Sid walked past Russ to the VCR and pushed EJECT. He had Russ figured two ways. One way, Russ didn't know Sid was involved, but it was only a matter of time before he started to add up the steering boxes and mobsters so that they equaled "Sleep." Who knows, he might even remember what Sid looked like standing in the glow of the burning car. So Sid figured the best thing was to take charge of the situation, to put a positive spin on what and how Russ learned.

Figuring Russ another way, it could be that he already knew Sid was involved, in which case Sid should find out Russ's motives for keeping quiet, however sinister. Sid decided he'd better stay near the hatchet, just in case.

What with the tape rescued, he had decided Russ was either primed for satisfaction, caught off guard, or both, any or all of which played to Sid's benefit. Sid held up the tape.

"It was this guy."

"Who?"

"The guy you ran down—he had rigged your wife's car. And I lied. His name wasn't Spaghetti. His name was Fest, and he was coming after me.

You killed him, you did me a favor." Sid stared into Russ's eyes a moment and flashed a smile. "But I didn't want to owe you one, I wanted you to owe me one for helping you get rid of the body." Sid picked up a newspaper and matches that were laying next to the woodstove.

"You're telling me this man Fest was...that he..." Russ ran a hand through his hair.

Sid was nodding solemnly, heading for the front door.

"And I killed him." Russ steadied himself with a hand on the wall. "I killed the guy who killed Sandra?" He felt like smiling. Or crying. The awakening from a white-knuckle nightmare, where passing realities sideswiped in bursts of sparks, left him groping in the dark for his vanquished burden. He wanted to hold it for a second longer and then let it go.

"That trick with the steering box, that I did with your truck to make it look like it failed? It was Fest that showed it to me. Same thing done to your wife's car. C'mon, let's step outside and burn this tape."

Sid pulled open the door.

They had company.

"Gimme the tape!" Price, face smeared with mud like a Navy SEAL on maneuvers, was squeezing Jenny around the throat with one arm. His other hand held a fish-cleaning knife. Behind him in the driveway stood the Bobs and Lloyd, cringing next to Big Bob's Bronco.

"Sid, just give him the tape," Little Bob implored.

Russ staggered to the doorway, and Sid pursed his lips, shifty eyes taking in the new situation and betraying his reluctance.

"I heard it. I heard you play the tape." Price twitched, blinking hard. "Now give it to me." He coughed, pressing the knife to Jenny's throat.

"Sid," Jenny hissed, flapping her yellow-slickered arms. "Give him th'damn tape, will ya please?"

"So your teacher tells me you've been skipping class, is this true, Penelope?" Warden Lachfurst had washed up and changed into Sid's quilted blue satin bathrobe. He brandished the small end of a fly rod.

"Maybe," Penelope said defiantly from the couch where she was perched. She'd put on one of Sid's white shirts, wrapped a dark blue plaid towel around her waist for a skirt, pulled on long white tennis socks, and put her hair in twin ponytails. It was just such lascivious encounters that had ushered her into doing tape in the first place.

"You know, this isn't the first time we've had to talk about your behavior." Lachfurst pointed his swagger stick at her. "And frankly, I wonder what we're going to do about you."

Lachfurst noticed muffled commotion outside, heard an outboard motor start, and then heard glass break, none of which drew his attention away from Penelope.

"Principal Lachfurst, what do you care whether I go to class? Huh? It's not like I'm your daughter or anything." Penelope crossed her legs.

"I care, Penelope, because I'm your principal, because your parents have entrusted me to take care of you, as if you were my own daughter." Some excited shouting, then several car doors slamming erupted in the distance. Penelope recrossed her legs, less conscious of the ruckus outside than her regret at not having a camcorder handy.

"So what are you gonna do about it? Send me to my room? Make me go to bed without supper?" She coyly bit a knuckle and looked sideways at the principal.

Lachfurst turned briefly to the window overlooking the river. He could see what looked like Fest in a motorboat, headed downriver.

He turned back and tapped Penelope's thigh with the rod tip. "What you really need is a good spanking."

"Oh, you'd like that, wouldn't you, Principal Lachfurst? I'll bet there's a lot of girls at the school you'd just love to paddle."

"You have a dirty mind, Penelope, and what I'm going to do is tell your parents about your absenteeism."

Penelope jumped to her feet.

"My parents? But why not just kick me off the field hockey team or revoke my smoking privileges? Oh please, don't tell my parents?!" she pleaded.

Lachfurst caught a glimpse out a side window of

a woman in a yellow rainsuit and Sid dashing by. Car doors opened and slammed in the side yard.

"No, I'm afraid I'm going to have to call your parents."

A car started, and the white LTD fishtailed up the drive.

"Please, Principal Lachfurst, not that, please! I'll do anything."

"I'm sorry, Penelope. Rules are rules. I have to be strict." Lachfurst stopped pacing and sat in an armchair.

Penelope stood and walked close in front of him, straddling his knees. "You wanna know what I was doing?"

Penelope glanced out the back window. Russ and Lloyd were in a motorboat headed downriver, Reverend Jim swooping alongside them.

"The case is closed, young lady."

"I was just going to tell you what I was doing. When I was playing hooky."

"A confession?"

"I was with Mona. She and I snuck off into the woods and played a little game." Penelope hiked her skirt up, just a little, which was a lot.

"A game?"

"Yes. What you do is you close your eyes, reach out, touch the person across from you with one finger, and just from that little contact try to tell what body parts you've touched. Have you ever played that game, Principal Lachfurst?"

"I can't say as I have."

"Here, try it. It's fun."

"Penelope, my mind is made up, I—"

"Here, I'll go first..."

Penelope put one hand over her eyes and reached out with the other. She smiled. She wasn't touching anything, but Mr. Lachfurst was.

"Why, Principal Lachfurst! That's your tongue!"

chapter

23

Jenny braced herself against the dash as the LTD's tires sang along one of 241's sharp curves.

"Sid, what the hell is goin' on? Day started out normal. Trailered my boat to the launch at Mink Run, put in, motored up to your place, and then this loony-toon jumps out of the bushes next to your house and takes me hostage. Now he's swiped my boat! And I don't much favor a knife to my throat or him pushin' me in the river." She wiped river water from her face.

"You need your boat, and we need that tape. Jenny, listen t'me here. Now's when we gotta keep our heads, all right? Think first and fast, be pissed off later. Where can we get in at the river?"

Jenny wiped at a rivulet running down her neck, glowered at the road, and said nothing.

"Are you thinking or what?" Sid prodded. "If you wanna get that boat, we gotta figure a way to grab him, either when he comes ashore or . . ."

"Hey." Jenny's eyes brightened. "Go straight here on 241." Her heart beat to the rhythm of the windshield wipers. "Sid, when ya was a kid, your dad ever take ya to the rodeo?"

"A what?" Sid glanced in the rearview mirror and noticed Big Bob's Bronco veer off behind them. "When I was a kid, the only place my dad took me was the woodshed. You got an idea?"

"Yup. Make a left at the railroad crossing."

The Bobs veered off at 383, headed for the bridge to New York.

"Where are they going?" From the passenger seat, Little Bob pointed at Sid's LTD barreling straight on 241.

"Hell, I dunno. Jenny's plenty angry, though. River's pretty cold this time of year to get dunked in it." Big Bob shrugged off a sympathy shiver.

"Couldn'ta missed the turn, and that way they're just gonna drive away from the river." Little Bob shook his head. "I don't get it."

"Well, what we gotta think about is what we're gonna do. So we drive down 79 on the New York side, follow him. Then what?"

Little Bob shrugged.

"He's gotta be headed somewhere, and when he gets there, he's gonna come ashore, right?"

"Yeah, well, we just better hope it's the New York side of the river, maybe right at Mink Run. We won't be able to cross again until we hit Frustrumburg."

The Bronco buzzed across the simple truss bridge spanning the Delaware River called the Mink Run Bridge. They slowed to a stop midcrossing.

"There he is, comin' this way." Big Bob tapped the glass, pointing.

"Wow, but I don't see Russ and Lloyd." Little Bob craned to see past Big Bob's bulk.

"They'll be along. Russ's motor's got ten horses, Jenny's got seven. They'll be along any—hey, there they come!"

A thousand feet upriver was Russ's boat in full-speed pursuit.

Big Bob drove the Bronco to the New York side of the bridge and pulled in to Mink Run's dirt lot and boat launch, right next to Jenny's pickup and trailer.

They got out and scrambled along a slippery path down to the river, headed for some boulders under the bridge at its pier. The drizzle had slackened to mist, and the sky was brightening.

Price looked at the bridge and the shore, then slowed his motor. Then he noticed the Bobs, throttled up, and zoomed on.

"There he goes," Little Bob moaned.

"Maybe we shoulda stayed up top, caught him when he landed. What do ya think?" Big Bob jerked a thumb back toward the Bronco.

"I think he's headed for Frustrumburg."

* * *

Price's mind was soaring on sleepless wings, empowered by greed, aloft in skies clouded by the persistent gong of a shovel blade bashing his parietal bone. The sutured bullet wound on his chest bled lazily.

"There's a whole lotta these people in on this thing. That woman, the old guy, the big guy, the little guy, the bearded guy—they're all in on it! Boy, maybe there's rewards for them. Maybe they're all fugitives."

Motoring toward the right shore, he cut the boat into a flume, glancing off a rock and wending through some rapids.

"Let's see, now the hundred grand will be all mine, and if you guess that, on average, each of the others gets me, say, five grand...Maybe I'll end up with a hundred twenty-five grand."

He tried to wipe some of the dried mud from his face with a filthy forearm. Sweat beaded on his brow.

"Lord knows how many people these folks have bumped off. They lure them up there, then run them over with trucks! Probably where the New York mobs dispose of people. Who would ever think of Hellbender Eddy! Ha! It's brilliant. Maybe that tough old bird's the ringleader."

Price saw something black coming at him in his peripheral vision and ducked—Reverend Jim swooped down and landed on the boat's bow. The boat swerved under some willow branches and veered back out toward the channel. The prop fouled briefly in the weeds, and he played with the throttle a moment to make sure the outboard kept running. He squinched his eyes shut and gave his brain a rattle. Sleep had been a stranger to him these past couple of days. Was that a one-legged bird sitting on the bow?

Reverend Jim considered Price with one eye, then the other, his head cocked in anticipation.

"Maybe I should just forget about calling Captain Reuster. Yeah, maybe I should just call the FBI. This is interstate, after all. Reuster, if I call him, he'll just laugh. Those bastards at the hospital! Ha! Try to keep me from my wife, will ya?"

His watery, feverish eyes scanned the shore, then focused on Reverend Jim. What did that damn bird want, anyway?

"Damn." Russ nodded at the bridge ahead. "I thought he was gonna pull over at Mink Run."

Lloyd looked downriver.

"The Bobs scared him off. But now where's he going to come ashore? Beyond here, he'll have to walk a mile or so or do some rock climbing to get outta the woods." Lloyd scratched his beard. "He can't be thinking about going to Frustrumburg."

"Can't he?" Russ snorted.

"But what about Peekamoose Falls?"

Widely known as the Delaware's most treacherous

rapids, Peekamoose Falls gave pause to even the most seasoned canoeists and kayakers. As the sides of the falls were comprised of unruly mobs of boulders, there was only one way through the rapids—right down the center, a quarter mile of unpredictable liquid maelstrom. Recreational boaters knew to take out at Mink Run to avoid the falls altogether. Though there were no sheer vertical drops along Peekamoose Falls, the remarkably turgid boils thundered downhill, aimed at one rock that stood out from the gangs to either side. Known as "The Moose," this towering boulder was the biggest, meanest, most igneous rock of them all, a drunken, belligerent bully who'd stepped out to face down all challengers.

Russ throttled back his outboard at the Mink Run Bridge, where signs to either side of the river warned boaters: "DANGER: IMPASSABLE RAPIDS—POINT OF NO RETURN."

Lloyd pointed downriver. "Is that Reverend Jim in the boat with him?"

"Jenny, I gotta tell you, this is nuts!" Sid looked up and down the tracks. "What should happen, if, like, a train comes?"

"Ya got any better ideas?" Jenny coiled rope around her forearm. "Besides, trains don't come along that often."

Sid heaved the rest of the rope out of the trunk of his LTD and slammed the lid. It was the same rope he'd used for dropping Fest's body down the pile casing. He and Jenny stood on a high, narrow steel and stone bridge with one track and no handrails.

"What, a train once a week, once a month, what?"

Jenny pointed an arresting finger. "Look, buster, you owe me one."

"How often?"

"Once a day or so."

"Once a day? Or so?"

"If a train comes, we'll pull off the tracks, O.K.?"

"Jenny, we're in the middle of a goddamn bridge here! Pull off where?" Sid gestured to the river below. "Into that mean-lookin' piece of river? I don't think so." He ran a hand through his hair, shaking his head at Peekamoose Falls far below. He knew he shouldn't be doing this, not with Jenny wearing those damned red hikers. Sid wasn't just tempting fate, he was baiting it.

Jenny cinched a slipknot in the rope and fixed a loop in the end. "We'll be outta here in no time, Sid. Don't be such a chickenshit." She tossed her lasso over an I beam and down the side of the trestle.

Sid glowered at her. "Can y'at least tell me which way the train comes, so I'm not, like, driving toward the friggin' thing as it comes at me?"

"From Frustrumburg, from New York, that direction." Jenny lashed her end of the rope to the bumper of the LTD. "Now get in the car and I'll tell ya when t'go."

"That direction?" Sid pointed, taking the opportunity to wipe sweat from his brow with a forearm. "You're sure?"

"Will ya get in the damn car, Sid? He's coming...."

"The train's comin'?" Sid prepared to run.

"No, Sid. Look, upriver. That fool with my boat is what's coming. Now get in the car." Jenny shoved him toward his charge.

Sid glanced skyward, where the sun seemed to have edged its way between the clouds so as not to miss the action. "What'd I do to deserve this?"

Actually, he could think of a few things.

Price hardly noticed the "POINT OF NO RETURN" signs, but he did notice the car above, the woman, and the snare. There was no real way around the rope's area of influence. It was evident to Price, even in his state, that any effort to avert a direct shot at the main channel would put him into some nasty-looking rocks. Peekamoose's roar blended with the shovel clanging in his head.

A lasso hung just three feet above the water. But there was nothing to keep Price from deflecting it, which, as he drew near, he prepared to do with an outstretched arm. If nothing else, he hoped the lasso would scare off that damn black bird that was circling above him.

Reverend Jim ducked under the loop as it passed over the bow, then seemed to sense trouble and took flight.

The loop approached Price's hand.

The loop went suddenly up, over his head.

Then down, behind him. It was a fake-out. The snare came down flat, and right over the outboard.

"Go!"

Sid could have sworn he heard a locomotive blast at some distant grade crossing. The LTD rolled five feet, and the rope snapped taut with a sound like the crack of a bullwhip.

Price was struggling to pull the snare back over the outboard's cowling when the rope lashed tight. The outboard punched him in the chest and a jolt folded him over the motor. His next, gasping sensation was like getting clonked over the head with a shovel again. Spinning, buzzing, floating. He caught a flash of the boat drifting pretty-as-you-please down the rapids. From above he heard a resounding shout.

"SHIT!" Jenny shouted again, stomping the gravel and kicking the ties with her crimson hikers. She leaned back over the bridge to reaffirm the disaster. Yup, there went her boat, drifting down Peekamoose Falls. Below dangled her motor, still sputtering on fumes, the fuel hose hanging down like a monkey tail, and Price draped over the top.

The idea had been to lift the boat by the engine and dump Price.

The rope crackled as it slid over the I beam, her catch-o-the-day twirling as he rose.

"Sid! Stop, Sid!" The LTD didn't stop. In fact, it sped up. "What the...?" Jenny propped a foot on a rail and her kneecap hummed. Steel rail plates clattered up and down the track.

"Oh, damn it to hell!" She took a few steps backward, turned, and hightailed it over the bridge toward New York.

"Jenny? Hey! Jenny!" Lloyd shouted from Russ's boat under where Price hung.

Russ had the boat pointed upriver, three-quarter throttle just to remain in place. He noted tiny bits of leachate and rust starting to fall from the trestle, dimpling the water.

"Uh-oh." Rope bristled over the I beam overhead as Price rose steadily into the air. Russ looked toward the Pennsylvania bank and saw the LTD's shadow on the swirling water, headed for shore.

"You hear that? Is that a...? That's a train!" Lloyd shouted. "When it rolls over the rope...if Jenny, or the car..." Lloyd looked over at the LTD's shadow.

Rail plates clanked above, while Price twirled and moaned.

* * *

A huge steel sphinx on wheels, the locomotive and a mile of freight cars quaked around the bend just as the LTD, trundling over the wood ties, reached a stone's throw from Pennsylvania. And just when Sid thought he was going to dodge the bullet, he took his eyes from the rearview mirror. The bend that the train was coming around was in Pennsylvania, dead ahead.

The gap was closing fast.

Sid stomped both feet on the brake.

"Drop the tape in the boat and we'll save you," Russ urged Price, who seemed on the verge of delirium as he dangled above.

Reverend Jim swooped out from under the railroad bridge and landed on Price's back. He made a clucking, chuckling sound and pecked at Price's ear.

"Jim!" Russ yelled at the bird. "No! Go away!"

Price groped at his ear. "My earring!"

The diamond gripped in his beak, the bird hopped off Price's back and glided away toward shore.

"Hey, Russ." Lloyd pointed toward the LTD on the bridge above. "What's Sid stopping for?"

Russ followed Lloyd's finger and saw the shadow of the LTD backing up. Price started spinning downward rapidly.

As if it wasn't hard enough driving backward fast in a Wal-Mart parking lot, it was nearly impossible on railroad tracks.

Sid's arms cramped as they tried to hold the steering wheel straight, and his vision was so violently jarred that he couldn't make out the train rolling toward him from the other end of the trestle. But he felt it.

Just as Lloyd was getting a hand on Price's windbreaker, the LTD clunkered overhead, and Price and the motor shot back up into the air with a protracted wheeze.

Russ paled. From Pennsylvania, a huge, dark shadow drew across the river. There was the sound of a thousand fingernails drawn across a blackboard, sparks cascading from the trestle, and braking train wheels above.

Russ throttled up to get clear of the impending catastrophe. His boat lunged upriver, and Lloyd fell back over his seat to the floor.

When the train was five feet away, Sid was able to make it out clearly enough. And when the locomotive's front rammed into the LTD's hood, there was a millisecond where Sid looked up and saw the engineer. He was wagging his head. "Not a chance," he seemed to be saying.

Sid cut the steering wheel—hard. And for a sweet, brief moment, the jarring, the vibration, the squealing metal, and the locomotive were gone. The moment lingered, as such moments of truth often do, long enough for Sid to flip back through all the red shoes to the very first ones pounding a Chevy window on a steamy nighttime Passaic River bulkhead.

Russ and Lloyd shook splashes of water from their arms and eyes, staring back slack-jawed at the calamity.

The LTD stood on its trunk end in some rocks at the rapids' edge, water up to the driver's door, sparks and splash raining down from above. The train was still thundering overhead when they motored up to the car. Only the frayed end of a rope still hung where Price and Jenny's motor used to be.

Lloyd grabbed hold of the LTD's fender when they pulled alongside, and the car groaned, tipping farther backward.

"Don't!" Russ shouted.

"I'm sorry, I'm sorry!" Lloyd yelped.

Russ nudged the boat up close to the car, and Lloyd tried to lean into the driver's window. He quickly withdrew.

"Can't." Lloyd flapped his arms in frustration. "Can't get the angle on him. Too heavy, and with my back ... And what if the car falls over?"

"Here, take the throttle."

They switched places, and Russ was soon assessing the situation through the open driver's window.

Blood was splattered on the fractured windshield and on Sid's face, which was held out of the water by the headrest. His eyes were partially open, and one hand pawed at the water indifferently.

"Sid! Sid, c'mon! Wake up! Gotta get outta there." Russ slapped him on an outstretched arm, then tugged his wrist.

Sid's eyes goggled a moment, and he gurgled.

"Sid!" Russ screamed.

Jerking his head forward, Sid let it splash back onto the headrest. He groaned, and his eyes rolled at Russ.

"Id was me dat..." he slurred, then smiled like a drunkard. "Y'still owe me, Russ."

"Sid! C'mon! Snap outta it!" Russ implored.

Pawing the air a moment, Sid groped the steering wheel in a vain attempt at pushing himself toward Russ.

"Y'owe me, Russ." He groaned. "You was in that wreck, an' I grabbed your, your..." Sid made a gun out of his hand and pointed it at Russ.

"Sid!" Russ had ahold of Sid's sleeve, and he pulled. The LTD groaned, twisting toward him. He could hear the trunk grinding into the river bottom. But the car stopped.

"Get me outta here," Sid pleaded, his eyes unable to focus, his hands slapping at the steering wheel.

"Russ," Lloyd shouted, "get the hell away from that car. It's going to go!"

The train overhead finally lumbered to a stop.

"Bring me right up to the car. I'll grab him, then I'll tell you when to back away."

Russ leaned far enough in to grab Sid by the collar.

"Russ, y'owe me, dammit, d'int y'understand." Sid's bloodshot eyes rolled aimlessly. "I pulled you from that wreck. The car was burning, you were, were..."

"Burning? The car...you mean in Connecticut?" Russ grabbed Sid by the collar, but not necessarily to save him.

Sid seemed to focus for a moment, at least with one eye.

"I pulled you away," he rasped, grinning. *"O.K., Evel Knievel, just keep your eyes and your mouth shut, and I'll save your sorry ass, you got that?"*

With a trembling lip, Russ glared hard at the bloodied face, the grin.

"Why? Why?"

Sid laughed, or coughed.

"She was a witness, Russ. She saw Fest whack Ristocelli..."

"So you killed Sandra?" Russ tightened his grip on Sid's collar and shook him. "Then why did you save me? Why didn't you let me die too?"

"Hurry, Russ!" Lloyd begged.

Sid started pushing at the steering wheel, but Russ pushed him back. Sid's eyes turned to slits as he tried to force his eyes to focus, his delirium waning.

"Fest put the fix on the steering box, I just followed to make sure the job was done, that's all. I maya killed a lot of people, Russ, but..." Sid smiled, and it was neither a grin nor a sneer. It was just a gentle smile of humility. "But sometimes even I can, y'know, I feel sorry for people." Sid tried to shrug. "Y'owe me that."

"*Owe you?*"

Without warning, the river pushed the car backward. This time it didn't stop.

If Russ had had the time to make a decision, he might well have let go of Sid's collar.

The LTD rolled as it went, the driver's window turning upward. Lloyd steered the boat away from the falling car, and Sid slipped right out of the car into the river.

Even then Russ considered letting Sid go. But he didn't.

chapter
24

Leaving his Karmann Ghia parked above at the guide rail, Omer Phillips had picked his way down the steep embankment to the river's edge. For some time, he just stood watch on a rock, opera glasses pointed upstream. Eventually, he folded the glasses away and readied the life preserver.

A discus throw put the preserver out just far enough. Omer tied off his end to a tree stump and let the victim beach himself.

The washing-machine effect of the rapids had scoured the mud from Price's face, hair, and clothes, but it was clear that a bout in the ring with "The Moose" had taken its toll. Exhausted, bashed, wheezing, and wild-eyed, Price was Wile E. Coyote after a bad day chasing the Road Runner. He lay in the shallows among the rocks, clinging to the rope absently.

"Hello, Mr. Price. Glad to see you could make it."

The swimming vision of Omer, umbrella on tweed forearm, looked cheerily down.

"You..." Price wheezed, "you took the tape."

"That's right. I was trying to help you."

"Help?" Price rasped.

"See where all this tape business has gotten you?"

Price got a smile going on one side of his face, and he patted the rectangular bulge in his windbreaker.

"It's not over...yet. I held on to the tape...all the way, rolling underwater, a big...*big* rock." Price almost passed out from the thought, but he coughed up some water and shook his brain awake. "I held on to...the tape."

"Admirable. But I'm afraid the tape is no good to you now." A glint of sun winked off Omer's eye and blinded Price. He held a hand over his eyes.

"It'll dry."

"That's not what I meant."

When Price lowered his hand, he saw Omer holding another tape. Omer addressed the question in Price's eyes.

"I'll give you this tape, for that tape."

Consternation knit Price's brow.

"You see, Mr. Price, this tape is of your wife and a man dressed as a cow engaged in a sexual liaison. Very entertaining. If you don't give me your tape, I'll see to it that certain acquaintances in, shall we say, the lower echelons of the pornography industry release it. In fact, the tape is so entertaining that

I shouldn't wonder that all your fellow troopers might enjoy a copy for their personal libraries."

Price clearly didn't understand. Omer knew he wouldn't, so he handed down a stack of still shots featuring Debbie and the cow.

Price's pupils shrank to pinholes.

chapter
25

"Dammit, officer, can't you see the man's incapacitated? He's been in a wreck, he has a concussion, contusions, broken bones, and a sprained neck. You heard the nurse. He needs rest."

Sid kept his eyes shut, feigning sleep, while Lachfurst was in the hallway reading the cops the riot act. There was some minor protestation.

"Your questions can wait until the man's had a chance to recover his senses, can't they? So come back tomorrow. He'll be here. You have my guarantee."

Footsteps shuffled off down the hall. Lachfurst came in and stood over Sid for a while. Whether he was staring at Sid or reading a magazine, Sid hadn't a clue. But a nurse came in, rolled Sid on his side, and jabbed something up his rectum. Talk about a pro. His eyes bulged, but he didn't make a peep.

"Nurse, are the results of the scan in yet? How's the man's brain?" Lachfurst zipped up his jacket.

She tapped a finger on Sid's hip as she awaited the result of the thermometer.

"You'll have to talk to the doctor about that, but I think it turned out he's O.K."

"Capital. I'll go locate the doc."

The nurse extracted the thermometer and left.

Sid lay still, listening to footsteps and whispers in the hall. When he finally figured the coast was clear, he opened one eye.

Jenny stood next to his bed, grinning.

"How ya doin', flyboy?"

He cleared his throat and spoke in a hoarse whisper.

"Just for your, you know, future reference and whatnot, the train comes from Pennsylvania, not from New York."

"Sorry 'bout that." Jenny winced. "Tell ya what. Let's just call it even, O.K.? Ya don't owe me anything."

Sid shook his head as best he could. He wore a neck brace and had numerous small sutures on his bruised forehead and nose. The gray at his temples seemed more so.

"No dice. You owe me, Trout Lady. Dinner."

"Great." Jenny produced a pizza box, pulled a slice out, and offered him a bite.

"This isn't exactly what I had in mind." Sid chomped at the pie.

"Don't forget, I maya got my boat back, and I maya fished out my motor, but, Sid, this hasn't exactly been a shad fest for me neither." Jenny took a bite of the slice and pulled a beer from her bomber jacket.

"Hey, I'm the one laid up in a hospital. Been layin' here for hours fakin' sleep. Didn't wanna talk to the cops until I had what the story was. What'd you guys tell 'em?"

"Just that some guy stole my boat, and that we came up with this kinda harebrained idea to drive onto the tracks and lasso the rascal." Jenny poured some beer into a sipping cup. "Never did find the guy. He maya drowned. But how about ya tell me the real story, Sid. What was all this crap about?" She put the straw up to Sid's lips.

Sid's slurping was interrupted by a gentle knock at the door. A tweeded man with an umbrella edged into the room.

"I do apologize for the intrusion, Mr. Bifulco, really." Omer approached, hat in hand. "I just thought you might want this." He held aloft a ziplock bag containing a badly melted SUPER*PROCAM tape. He set it next to the flowers on the table.

"After today's trials and adventures, I thought this would surely set your mind at ease." Omer beamed at the couple. "I took the liberty of heating it to the point of destruction."

Sid squinted, at the tape first, then the stranger.

"Do I, uh, know you?"

"I don't think so. How are things with Mr. Smonig? Well, I hope? Friendly? I'd heard he'd had an accident. Some faulty steering. But I trust he is steered clear of trouble now? I hope so. I think you've both had enough of that, as it were."

Sid ran a tongue along his teeth, still squinting.

"Yeah, well, Smonig's just great, and I think you could say he's got all his steering problems worked out. Nothing to worry about there."

"Ahem, fellahs, don't mind me, but what the hell are ya talking about?" Jenny had about as much intrigue as she could take. Her arms were folded and her foot was tapping.

Omer doffed his crusher, tipped it to the lady, and bowed out.

"Sid, who was that character? I think I've been just a little too damned easy on your privacy, that's what. Ya tell me right now, Sid: What is all this shit about? Either that or you're gonna owe me. And boy, do I mean owe me." Jenny rubbed her palms together greedily.

Sid eyed the ziplock with the tape in it.

"It was all about that."

"Is that what you guys were after? What was on that tape?" Jenny poked it with a finger.

Sid cocked an eye at Jenny and fleetingly reflected as to how Fest had had nothing to do with putting the jinx on Sandra's steering box.

"I think it's what they call, uh..." He snapped his fingers. "Pathetic Justice."

chapter
26

Herding back over Little Hound Mountain, the day's gaggle of clouds migrated to an orange sun. Stragglers, low dense puffs of mist, descended on the Delaware, flocks roosting for the evening, alighting on Hellbender Eddy. Cool air riding riffles streamed into the bay, swirling the diaphanous vapor. Twilight arcs penetrated from above. Wet bark, stone, and evergreen scents beckoned from the embankment.

Pink Creek steadily sirened a silky solo. Spring peepers piccoloed from a stand of buckbean, and black crickets celloed from the confines of a stump. A lone pickerel frog trumpeted from a submerged clump of leaves. Wraiths of mist waltzed slowly by.

Like a tiny red firefly, the ember of Phennel Rowe's Virginia Slims glowed in the shadows. She sat on a boulder, one hand propped on the handle of her shovel. A bucket of writhing lampers was at her side. Though Reverend Jim had spent the late afternoon overseeing her excavations in Pink Creek, he had disappeared as soon as the sun dipped over the hill.

Phennel smoked only on occasion, and a good harvest of lampers was one such occasion. It had developed into a fine spring evening, and as she shared a quiet moment with the darkening woods and listened to night settle in, she spied something coming through the mist in the river.

Downy petticoats of vapor rolled to either side of Russ as he paddled his boat gently into the Eddy.

Dusk deepened, the warm shadow of the woods absorbing the twilight. Though images of the ghostly cotillion and Pink Creek's ripple had lost definition, fading hues radiated in contrast, and the world in the Eddy was all-moving, a waterscape rendered in pixilated expressionist strokes.

There was no dimpling, tailing, or rising, and there was no reason that the trout would necessarily still be there, much less feeding. It had been years since Russ had fished Pink Creek. But when he awoke that afternoon from a deep sleep, he somehow knew a trout was waiting for him there. Russ watched in the flickering light as his fly line looped out behind. His wrist brought his forearm down, line and leader pulled the fly forward. Cartwheeling gently, the fly came upright and sat high on a riffle, right where it belonged, a dark speck on a distant mirror.

And just as though it had been rehearsed, the shiny speckled snout rose on cue. A delicate hushed rise took the fly. Tail and dorsal porpoised. The trout took its meal down.

The rod raised deliberately brought the line taut, and after a moment of realization, the trout drove toward the creek. Peepers and crickets ceased playing, and Pink Creek seemed to rush along to the drumbeats of blood in Russ's ears.

Racing in circles, the fish ran up into the creek mouth, fly line chopping fog swirls in two.

Suddenly the fish stopped, and in that instant, full night descended.

Russ didn't know what had happened at first. Maybe the trout wrapped the line around a log, or snagged it under a rock. But it started moving again and the action was different, a sleepy, side-to-side motion that came toward him from the creek. This was a different fish. The trout was gone, and Russ was attached to something heavy, something deep, something with a big head. It came right along toward the boat. Russ dropped the anchor with the flip of a switch. Nervous hands ransacked one of the boat's cubbyholes for a flashlight that wasn't there.

At first, as Russ coaxed the fish up and saw the silhouette, he thought it was a giant bullhead catfish. Driving the net into the water, he scooped, groping in the dark to get it all in the mesh pocket.

A tremendous splash divulged a gaping mouth from which his original trout sprang and slapped him in the jaw. Two feet kicked wildly in the air, and a long, flat tail reached out and smacked Russ in the forehead, knocking him back.

Lying on the wet carpet in the bottom of his boat, he wiped the water and slime from his face, eyed the empty net beside him. The trout flopped and shuddered somewhere at the other end of the boat. He realized that his trout had been swallowed up by a hellbender.

Russ barked a laugh of disbelief, hauled himself up to the gunnel, and stared at the growing ring of dark ripples where the hellbender had vanished. Yes, yes, there were two feet, and that unmistakable wrinkled tail that had slapped the side of his head. A hellbender. He'd really seen one. He couldn't wait to tell...

Staring up at holes parting in the mists, at the stars above, Russ suddenly realized that the weight of his burden was gone. Was it that he'd killed the guy who killed his wife and that justice had been done? Was that what had really mattered all along anyway? Wasn't most of the lingering pain associated with being the survivor of the accident, and not knowing why?

Sid said he'd felt sorry for him, but Russ doubted that motivation. Sid obviously had the sense to give Russ the only acceptable reason: compassion. Was it compassion that made Russ hold on to Sid's shirt-front and not let go?

Russ couldn't come up with a reason for saving Sid, so how could he expect Sid to have a reason for saving Russ? Perhaps, Russ thought, there was no

percentage in trying to assign significance to everything that happens to you.

Russ stared down at the dark water where the
huge salamander had vanished, seeing his rippled
silhouette haloed in stars against the night sky.

He had dwelled all afternoon on his new understanding of Sandra's predicament. Russ understood
now that Sandra had witnessed a mob hit and had
never told him, never told anyone—and yet was
killed anyway. Why had she never told him? He
guessed the same reason he wouldn't have told her.
To protect her.

And sort of in honor of that, or perhaps to share
something with Sandra, he decided never to tell anyone about the hellbender.

He smiled, looked up at the stars, and considered
what Phennel would say about all this.

"Hallelujah," he said aloud.

"Amen," echoed back from the woods.

ABOUT THE AUTHOR

BRIAN M. WIPRUD is a New York City author and outdoor writer for fly-fishing magazines. He won the 2002 Lefty Award for Most Humorous Crime Novel, was a 2003 Barry Award Nominee for Best Paperback Original, had a 2004 Independent Mystery Booksellers Association Bestseller, and a 2005 *Seattle Times* Bestseller. Information on his tours and appearances can be found at his website www.wiprud.com.

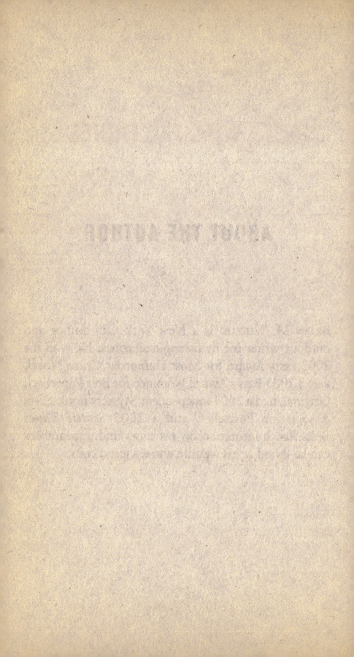

If you enjoyed

SLEEP WITH THE FISHES

don't miss
the newest crime caper from
"sublime comic genius"

BRIAN M. WIPRUD

Read on for an exclusive
sneak peek at
his next mystery

coming from Dell Books
in Summer 2007.

Pick up your copy at your favorite bookseller.

chapter 1

Driving into Chicago at five o'clock on a Wednesday afternoon is like entering a circle in hell—possibly one sandwiched between the Pit of a Hundred Thousand Root Canals and the Fiery Baths of Microwaved Cheese. Yes, it was a crisp blue June day, and there the Lincoln and I were stuck in the Canyon of Interminable Cross Merges. New York is no treat at that time of day, either, but it's merely a stroll through bunny-soft purgatory by comparison, believe you me.

I'd meant to slip in just before rush hour, but construction on the interstate in Gary, Indiana, had held me up on my way from visiting my mom in Ann Arbor. Well, at least I could be grateful I wasn't in Gary anymore.

My course was set to see a bear. A Chicago Bear,

to be precise. Sprunty G. Fulmore was a running back in the midst of a gazillion dollar contract with the venerable ursine NFL franchise. He could also afford to be a big-game trophy hunter in the off-season. It's an expensive undertaking to bag Africa's big five: lion, elephant, rhino, leopard, and hippo. It requires special permits, top guides at top lodges, prep and export fees, and a whole gamut of red tape that only the rich can untangle with a few snips from cash's giant green scissors. But the expenses don't stop there—it's also none too cheap to have an elephant's head mounted. And of course you have to have the kind of palatial abode with space enough to hang one of those suckers and not make it look like it's crashing through the wall.

But the inventory of Mr. Fulmore's trophies, which I carried in my briefcase, included a lot more than those five animals. He had an appallingly large collection of dead stuff—culled from five continents—for a man in his early thirties.

Yes, Garth Carson carrying a briefcase. My taxidermy rental days weren't behind me, just to the side—I no longer spent my time working the angles to drum up business since it interfered with my new job appraising taxidermy collections for Wilberforce/Peete, a specialty insurance company that caters to the rich and famous' taste for collecting. How did I land this peachy gig? For once my brother Nicholas had brought sunshine to my life rather than forbidding black clouds. He's an insurance investigator, and had given me some connections. Before the insurance work, I'd been more or less just holding my own, my nose pressed against the glass ceiling. I'd no idea insurance companies needed people with my expertise. Or how well they paid. Because of this surge in profits, Angie and I now owned our apartment. At forty-six, my midlife-crisis days were well behind me. Every time I looked at that briefcase, a big smile spread across my face.

My Danger Days were behind me too. There had been a period when I just couldn't seem to stay out of trouble—with the criminal element or with the law. It had been two blissful years since the last episode, since anybody had tried to kill me. And by the looks of things, I was free and clear.

Okay, so maybe not so free and clear since I was now fighting my way across six lanes of the Indy 500 trying to make the Wacker Drive exit. But I'm a New Yorker. I simply bullied my way across the interstate, leaned on my horn and cut everybody off. Tires screeched and legions of irate Chicagoans flipped me the bird, their lips pantomiming expletives. The scariest part was that a disproportionate number of them actually looked like their patron saint, Mike Ditka.

I'd never been to Chicago before. Downtown seemed much like parts of Manhattan but with mostly named streets. It's just that there was a river cutting through part of it, and I had a little trouble getting across it to where my hotel was. Soon enough, though, I was in the semicircular driveway of the glass monolith, a cadre of valet parking guys eyeing my car with the thinly disguised trepidation of cowpokes approaching a fiery bull. I was used to this. To these twenty-five-year-old kids, my black '66 Lincoln convertible, with its giant steering wheel, knobs, and tranny hump was an alien, unpredictable thing. Other than some SUVs, cars haven't been made this heavy or this long since way before these dudes were born.

As the bellhops unloaded my gear from the trunk, I eyed the oldest valet. "You ever drive a vintage ride like this?"

He paused, and did so too long.

The youngest of the bunch piped up.

"My gramps has a '72 Eldorado. Drove it to Vegas last summer. She made wide turns, you know?"

"Circle gets the square." I tossed him the keys.

"Dope!" He smiled. "Circle gets the what?"

"Forget it." I tucked a twenty in his shirt pocket as he moved toward the driver's seat. "Car's got a new paint job so be nice to her."

I followed the bellhops into the shiny building, did all that check-in stuff, and by 6:00 p.m. I was laying on the bed in my shiny room. Then the phone rang.

"This Carson?" a man's voice asked.

"Who's this?"

"Wilberforce/Peete, right?"

"Yes. Is this Mr. Fulmore?"

"Yeah, that's me. Car'll pick you up in an hour. Howzat?"

"Sounds fine."

"That's cool. I'll leave the front door open. See you in a few."

"Sure."

I'll be the first to admit that I have a prejudiced perspective on big game hunters because my work seems to bring me eyeball to eyeball with the worst of them. But a lot has changed since midcentury when trophy hunting was done without conscience or forethought. True sportsmen today are equal part conservationists, promoting sustainable-use programs and contributing to international efforts to keep the populations of game animals healthy enough so that they can continue to kill them. I know, it sounds counterproductive, but I guess it's the Omelet Theory in action, and they're breaking a few eggs. Argue that it would be better to hatch the eggs if you must, but there's no denying that these big game hunters channel a lot of money, effort, and influence toward conservation efforts that otherwise wouldn't be there. For example, the biggest, oldest, and most venerable award in trophy hunting used to be called the Oglevy Cup and was awarded to the hunter with the most spectacular kill. Today, that same award is called the Oglevy Conservation Award and is given to the hunter who has contributed the most toward improving the sport—i.e., keeping the animals around. Hats off to the nature lovers who do their bit, but the luminaries of big game hunting do their bit and then some.

For obvious reasons, most of the big game hunters I visited were eager to try to grease my wheels. They wanted the highest appraisal possible, if not for insurance reasons, then for bragging rights. If they ever got into a pissing contest with other hunters, even if they didn't have a saber-toothed wombat or hoary tree kangaroo among their trophies, they could always pull the trump card by announcing how much their collection was worth. Sad, really. True collectors such as myself tend not to be competitive on that scale—we're more apt to be kindred spirits, appreciating the sensibilities evidenced in someone else's collection. Taxidermy is art. But with hunters, their "trophies" were exactly that: a show of prowess.

My motto? Don't let other people make their problems yours. If these guys wanted to smoke cigars, drink sixty-year-old Scotch, and lock horns over whose dead animals were bigger, better, or worth more money, let them have at it. Besides, it benefited me. Whenever I visited these big game hunters, they wined and dined me, sent cars, and lavished me with Cuban cigars I didn't smoke—it was only the gold watches and home entertainment systems that Wilberforce/Peete forbade me to accept. And of course, these erstwhile Hemingways, knowing I was exposed to some of the finest trophy collections, wanted me to be their magic mirror and tell them theirs was the finest in all the land.

An hour after Fulmore's call, I was in a limo headed for an upper-crust Chicago suburb. And I couldn't help but reflect, once again, how dramatically my life had changed in a year. Nothing highlights the notion that you're no longer treading water than having the captain send out his launch for you. Pipe me aboard! I was liking this new life. A lot.

Once off the highway, we cruised through a Tudor-style retail strip and into a lane canopied by the thick branches of towering sycamores. Portico lights twinkled through the hedgerows.

It was obviously trash night in Upper Crust, Illinois. You know you're in a schmancy neighborhood when all the houses have matching trash cans—the clean green PVC kind with rubber wheels, whisper-quiet hinged lids, and no house numbers spray painted on the sides. I'd bet the garbage trucks were electric and the sanitation workers wore matching white jumpsuits and sneakers so as not to wake anybody. Like the tooth fairy, the rubbish fairies fluttered in and out without so much as causing a head to lift from its pillow.

The chauffeur slowed as we approached a drive with a white lawn jockey next to it. For the uninitiated, a drive is distinguished from a driveway by the semicircular, dual entrance design that obviates having to use reverse gear. When you think about it, the less you have to use reverse gear the richer that means you are. Any place you would shop has valet parking where you just pull straight up to the entrance and somebody else parks and retrieves your car. You don't have to park in the regular parking spaces at the Foodco because you no longer food shop—your staff does. If you have a garage, somebody brings the car "around for you." And eventually, you just stop driving altogether—why even risk having to use reverse in an emergency? All that bothersome neck and head twisting. That's what you pay a personal trainer for, after all.

Passing a sea of green stuff—it was way too neatly trimmed and uniform to be grass—the limo approached a Georgian façade: red brick, white pillared portico, ivy, dormers. I had to remind myself I wasn't dropping in on a bank president, but a running back named Sprunty who probably favored wild pool parties awash in cheerleaders and controlled substances. I could only imagine the fuss his neighbors had made when he'd signed the deed to this mansion. But that was their problem. Not mine.

The limo rolled to a stop in front of the portico and the driver killed the engine. This wasn't like calling a town car in New York. Here, a limo would wait, no matter how long. And instead of some surly Balkan malcontent sharing his highly original views on impromptu capital punishment to the accompaniment of a radio blaring balalaika disco, my driver hadn't said a word the whole trip. If he was Bosnian or Croatian, I had no idea. He could even been Hutu or Tutsi. I didn't notice.

My briefcase and I stepped out of the limo, and from the portico's vantage I surveyed the sea of green. Fireflies looped and blinked their way through the vapor looking for their mates. Toads chirped.

Crickets cheeped. As somnolent a June evening as ever there was.

I turned to the door, which was about six feet wide. When Sprunty had said on the phone that he'd leave the door open, I thought he meant unlocked. But it was open open.

"Mr. Fulmore?" My voice bounced up and around the soaring entryway like a Super Ball. An Escheresque staircase stood directly ahead, so long it should have been an escalator. "Hello?"

No butler or housekeeper in evidence. I stepped into the foyer. "Hello?"

On my right was a living room, all in white, with lots of plants and nothing on the walls. To my left was an open door that led to an oak-paneled library, the kind you'd think more appropriate for John Houseman than Fulmore. Ahead, to the right of the stairs, was a white door held partially open by a bear's paw.

Bear's paw?

"Mr. Fulmore?" I strode over to the paw, which was lying on the floor. It was nearly the size of a baseball mitt, with claws like golf tees. Had to be Kodiak. I pulled the door open—it was one of those spring-loaded jobs that swung both ways, and it led into a pantry. Attached to the paw was the bear's forearm, and I picked it up with both hands. By the looks of the stump, it had been hastily cut from its mount. A few feet ahead was a large red puddle. I froze. Then I looked closer.

A woman's slip. And beyond that? A large brassiere, also red. I'm no expert, but I'd guess it was a 38D. Okay, so what man at forty-six doesn't have some knowledge of bras?

I didn't like the looks of this. The trail led to a door on the far side of the pantry. Beyond? The red panties, no doubt. I grimly surmised Sprunty was in rut, and I didn't want to be the one to turn the hose *au deux d'amor.*

So the bear arm and I beat a retreat to the living room, where I sat upon a couch that looked like it had never been sat on, neatening up the contents of my briefcase: a calculator, some lined legal pads, twenty-five-cent pens, a date book, some bottled water, and a box of Milk Duds. Maybe not exactly the contents of Donald Trump's attaché, but I'm told he does like the occasional Milk Dud.

Also contained within was a stack of papers Angie had handed me before I left. It was a dossier of dog breeds. I'd been avoiding reading through it all because I wasn't sure I really wanted a dog—but Angie seemed dead set on acquiring a canine to share our digs. We already had Otto, our jack-of-all-trades, and he was like a dog, wasn't he? Better still, I didn't have to chase him down the street with a Baggie on my hand, picking up his warm, moist loafs from the pavement. On the other hand, I felt a wee bit guilty. Angie and I had opted not to have kids, and if she felt the urge at this late stage for a third party, how could I refuse her a fur bearin' critter?

One that wasn't stuffed, that is. Sighing, I started flipping through the info on midsized to small terriers. Jack Russell, Wire Fox, Schnauzer... but it was hard to stay focused.

I couldn't imagine Sprunty hadn't heard me enter. Surely when he was finished slipping the wood to that cheerleader he'd come looking for me. He wouldn't want to keep his appraiser waiting long. I might get testy.

After half an hour of looking for the least objectionable mutt, I was getting impatient. If I had a cell phone, I would have called somebody. The bear arm was beginning to worry me too. Why would Sprunty cut the arm off his own bear mount, and right before an appraisal? Was it possible he'd cut it off somebody else's trophy on a wager or something?

Weary of the delay, I determined to barge in on them. Half an hour was long enough for him to have done what he needed to do. Now they were probably just in there having cosmos and cheese curls or something.

I pushed through the door at the far end of the pantry. When the door swung closed behind me, I was in darkness, awash in ripples of aquamarine, enveloped in the hushed silence of wall-to-wall carpeting. Across a sizeable room and beyond a gargantuan sectional sofa was a large array of sliding glass doors leading to a patio and lighted pool. That's it—they must be out by the pool.

But moments later I was outside standing next to

the blue glow of the pool. No Sprunty. No cheer-leader. No panties. Just the frogs and crickets chirping away.

I walked back through the sliding doors and felt along the wall for a light switch. Suddenly, Sprunty's trophy room blazed all around me. I could see that it extended almost the full width of the house, with dark paneled walls, white cathedral ceilings, white wall-to-wall shag, and white upholstered furniture.

Fulmore certainly had bragging rights. The pieces on the wall were mostly exotic, many full-bodied, and few of them small. A brooding black cape buffalo the size of a Cooper Mini was parked in one corner, a gnu at full gallop charging out from another. Along one wall, three rows of gazelle heads were arranged by size like some taxonomic display. There were mountain goats standing on fake rocks in the room's center, a lion jumping a Grants gazelle beyond that. Elk, moose, and rhino up there, an eight-hundred-pound black marlin up over there. A snarling polar bear clawed the air to the left of the stone fireplace, a cougar jumped a pronghorn by the bar, and a wolf gnashed its teeth over the door. It was like one of those sporting goods megastores. Taxidermy overkill. Or just plain overkill.

My eyes finally locked onto the Kodiak bear, which was standing in the corner to my right, his elbows stirring the air. Both forearms were missing, and I only held one of them in my hand. What kinda nut cuts both the arms off of his own trophy?

The Kodiak was helping the polar bear flank the

fireplace on the far side of a large sectional couch. To get there, I sauntered around behind the sectional, around the mountain goats, and in front of the bar. Ahead I saw something red.

Ah, the panties. I reached down to pick them up.

But what I encountered was wet. It was two dimensional. It was a stain.

My eyes swam—it must be red paint, cranberry juice, grenadine, Campari, raspberry syrup...but then the metallic bite of blood stung my nose.

I found my back pressed against the front of the bar, my hand reaching for the phone next to the beer taps. Fumble: Carson knocks the whole phone off the bar and onto the floor behind it.

"Nine one one, nine one one..." I was afraid I might forget the number as I stumbled behind the bar in search of the phone.

I stumbled, all right.

Onto Sprunty.

He'd been mauled by a bear. How'd I know? Sure, those gashes in his chest could have been made by a knife. But Fulmore's intestines were wrapped around the Kodiak's missing arm.

There was blood everywhere, and I almost slipped as I reached for the phone next to his head. I was averting my eyes from the gore, my breath coming fast, grunting with disgust, when I grabbed Sprunty by the nose by accident. His eyes, thankfully, were mostly closed. But his mouth was open. Something white was sticking out of it. A lizard? No, a gecko, probably a common house gecko. Dead too? I didn't know, I didn't care.

I grasped the phone and wheeled back around to the other side of the bar, falling to my knees on the clean white carpet. I misdialed three times before I got it right.

That was the day Sprunty's problems became mine.